Praise for Maria Grace

"Grace has quickly become one of my favorite authors of Austen-inspired fiction. Her love of Austen's characters and the Regency era shine through in all of her novels." **Diary of an Eccentric**

"Maria Grace is stunning and emotional, and readers will be blown away by the uniqueness of her plot and characterization" **Savvy Wit and Verse**

"Maria Grace has once again brought to her readers a delightful, entertaining and sweetly romantic story while using Austen's characters as a launching point for the tale." **Calico Critic**

I believe that this is what Maria Grace does best, blend old and new together to create a story that has the framework of Austen and her characters, but contains enough new and exciting content to keep me turning the pages. ... Grace's style is not to be missed.. **From the desk of Kimberly Denny-Ryder**

THE *Darcys'*
FIRST

Maria Grace

White Soup Press

Published by: White Soup Press

The Darcys' First Christmas
Copyright © December 2015 Maria Grace

For information, address
author.MariaGrace@gmail.com

ISBN-10: 0692590463
ISBN-13: 978-0692590461 (White Soup Press)
Author's Website: RandomBitsofFaascination.com
Email address: Author.MariaGrace@gmail.com

Dedication

For my husband and sons.
You have always believed in me.

Chapter 1

HAPPY FOR ALL HER maternal feelings was the day on which Mrs. Bennet got rid of her two most deserving daughters. The first Saturday in November, 1812, marked the day she ceased fearing the hedgerows and began talking of her daughters, Mrs. Bingley and Mrs. Darcy.

Elizabeth and Darcy spent the initial week of their marriage at his London townhouse and then set off for Pemberley, determined to spend their first Christmastide in the place he best loved.

Three days traveling gave Elizabeth plenty of time to nurse her anxiety over her new duties as mistress of Pemberley. Though Darcy insisted Mrs. Reynolds would ensure the transition was an easy one, Elizabeth struggled to share his sanguine outlook

.

Two days after they arrived, Elizabeth embarked upon her first day as mistress to the great estate. Meeting with the housekeeper, Mrs. Reynolds, was her first order of business.

She checked her hair in the looking glass and straightened her dress for the third time. There was no reason for disquiet, none at all. It was not as if she were preparing to make her curtsey for the King.

In many ways, though, that would be far less demanding. At court, she need only curtsey and remember all the steps and lines for her performance. Nothing more. But here …

She smoothed the hairs on the back of her neck. Darcy assured her she had nothing to fear from Mrs. Reynolds.

Little did he understand the complex and dynamic relationship between the mistress of the house and her housekeeper. No doubt Mrs. Reynolds was well aware she had not been raised to manage an estate the size of Pemberley. Mama had taught her well, to be sure. Yet, Longbourn was naught to the vast manor and thriving village that now looked to her to oversee, provide, nurture, educate …

How could she ever undertake such a task? Why did Darcy ever think her up to the challenge? He believed in her, insisted she was capable of anything she set her mind to, a bit like Papa. But perhaps, this once, his confidence was misplaced.

The clock chimed. Like it or not, it was time. Mrs. Reynolds would be waiting, and she was nothing if not punctual.

Elizabeth wove her way to the back of the manor. At least she no longer required directions to move from one room to another. The accomplishment felt far more impressive than it actually was. After all, even the lowest scullery maid managed the same undertaking with little effort.

What a grand achievement with which to begin her career as Mrs. Darcy!

The housekeeper's office, tucked at the rear of the house, near the kitchen, resembled Mrs. Reynolds herself, tiny, tidy and treasured. Along one wall, shelves held stacks of neatly folded linens, on another, rows and rows of sparkling china and crystal. A perfectly clean window kept sharp winter breezes at bay while a small fire warmed the room to cheeriness. A little plate of Elizabeth's favorite biscuits invited her to the table where Mrs. Reynolds presided over a large pile of books.

How had Mrs. Reynolds known those were her girl-hood favorites?

Several sheets of paper lay spread on the desk before her. Mrs. Reynolds squinted through her spectacles and hummed a tune under her breath, checking items off a list.

"Mrs. Darcy." Mrs. Reynolds rose and curtsied.

"Good morning, Mrs. Reynolds." The greeting sounded far more confident than she felt, not at all a difficult feat.

Mama insisted the better part of confidence was in one's voice. If one sounded confident, they were half way to being believed competent.

That might work for most people. Somehow, it did not seem Mrs. Reynolds would be so easily persuaded.

Elizabeth sat across from Mrs. Reynolds. A cool sunbeam shone over her shoulder and on the intimidating pile of journals and ledgers.

"Where do you recommend we begin?"

"Where do you prefer?" Mrs. Reynolds opened several books and laid them out along the length of the table, tapping each one in turn. "Menus are needed for the coming weeks. Laundry is planned for next week—you might wish to review our ways to confirm they meet your satisfaction. Perhaps you would care to go over the newly revised inventory of the larder? Meats just came from the smoke house and there are hams curing yet. The maids are preparing to change out the curtains for the winter. Would you care to inspect their efforts?"

Gracious heavens! So many books and lists.

Elizabeth rubbed her temples. "I have no idea."

Mrs. Reynolds pressed her lips and nodded. "It is a great deal to manage, is it not? Lady Anne—the late Mrs. Darcy—found it quite daunting at times, especially during the visiting months when company would fill every guest room. Oh, she loved the house parties, but between you and me, Missus, the work would overwhelm her sometimes."

"Indeed?"

"Absolutely. I kept a ready supply of willow bark for her headaches and mint for her digestion. She considered her brother, now Earl Matlock and sister, Lady Catherine, particularly ... challenging guests."

"Mr. Darcy has never mentioned it."

"His late mother never showed a sign of distress to her family or her visitors. She faced the trials with every imaginable grace, but make no mistake, it weren't easy for her"

"Oh."

Not the most original of responses, to be sure. But when one received intelligence that changed everything she believed about the world, more creative replies were out of the question.

"You never saw a more attentive mistress than her. She was well loved, indeed. Except by those who tried to take advantage of her. They found her rather disagreeable, I would think. She did not suffer fools or cheats lightly." She cocked her head and lifted an eyebrow. "I don't expect you would either."

Elizabeth chuckled. "I suppose you are right."

"Pemberley has run for a long time now without the hand of a mistress. Pemberley, she needs one. I done the best I could, but it ain't the same."

"No one criticizes your service, at least not to me."

"Of course not, I would box their ears if I heard of it!" Mrs. Reynolds threw her head back and laughed.

How delightful that the servants here laughed. A house needed laughter to truly be a home.

"Still, it is good for a mistress to preside over the household again. The master, he knows the land and the tenants, but the house—that has always been a mystery to him."

"I fear it may be a bit of a mystery to me as well."

Mama would scold her for revealing so much uncertainty to her staff, even though she regularly confided in Hill. But then, Mama had Hill's respect. Would she ever have Mrs. Reynolds'?

"A clever girl like you will have it sorted out in no time at all. I have no doubts." She caught Elizabeth's gaze, though it was entirely improper for her to be so bold.

The dear woman believed every word she said.

"I know the master well enough. He could not tolerate a stupid woman. Only a very clever one would make him as happy as he is now. You have nothing to worry about, Mrs. Darcy. It will come to you. All you need is a little time."

Elizabeth swallowed hard. The approval of a servant, even a senior, trusted one like Mrs. Reynolds, should not be so meaningful.

But it was.

"I have just the place to start." Mrs. Reynolds ambled around the desk to a plain cabinet under the window. "Here it is!"

She returned with a worn, red journal and handed it to Elizabeth.

Elegant, flourished handwriting greeted her as she opened it. "Whose?"

"Lady Anne's common place book. She would have wanted you to have it."

Elizabeth stroked the fine lettering. Darcy's mother had written this. She flipped through the pages. Receipts, garden plans, directions for her favorite wash balls …

"Oh!"

Mrs. Reynolds leaned over her shoulder. "She made lovely sketches, did she not? Quite a number of them are framed in the house. I will point them out to you when you wish. That one," she tapped the page, "that is the master when he was just five years old. Such a serious boy he was, but so kind hearted, even then. See here, she says it herself."

Fitzwilliam is the dearest of souls. He picked flowers for me this morning. I did not have the heart to tell him he pillaged my kitchen garden. Cook will be happy to know she will have far fewer courgettes to deal with this year. She considers them a most disagreeable vegetable.

Elizabeth giggled. A young Darcy's earnest eyes peered out from the page over a ragged bouquet in his hands.

He had not changed very much.

"It is good to hear you laugh, Missus." Mrs. Reynolds smiled a maternal smile. "Take that, and get acquainted with Pemberley through her eyes. Tomorrow is soon enough for the menus."

"Thank you, I will." Elizabeth gathered the book and pressed it to her chest.

How many times had she wished she could have known Darcy's mother, and through her, know him just a little better. Perhaps now, she could.

"I will be in my dressing room."

"Shall I send a tea tray up for you and … Lady Anne?"

"That would be lovely … and perhaps send this plate of biscuits as well?" Elizabeth picked up a biscuit and nibbled it.

"Those were her favorite, you know." Mrs. Reynolds trundled out.

Elizabeth made her way to her dressing room. How pleasant it would be to spend the rest of the morning taking tea with such a welcome guest. Perhaps, with the guidance of Pemberley's former mistress, she would be able do the role justice after all.

Several days later, after meeting with Mrs. Reynolds, Elizabeth made her way to the morning room. Menus were slowly coming together, as were plans for their Christmastide house party. The Gardiners and their children planned to arrive a week before Christmas. They would be easy guests to entertain, ready to be pleased with everything they saw. The perfect company for her inaugural holiday season.

Moreover, Aunt Gardiner's keen sense of style and propriety would identify anything still wanting in her hospitality. Her gentle spirit would deliver her pronouncements with far greater kindness than anyone else. Elizabeth anticipated her appraisals as much as her society.

The remainder of the day would be spent riding the estate with Darcy, calling on tenants and familiarizing herself with their families and needs. Longbourn's tenants were so few, they could be visited in a single day. Not so Pemberley's.

Papa had always praised her excellent memory. She would definitely need it today. That and the little notebook tucked in her basket. With Mrs. Reynolds' assistance, she had already established a page for each farm and family on the estate.

Darcy waited in the morning room, hidden behind his newspaper.

He rose as she entered. "Good morning, Mrs. Darcy."

She curtsied.

No it was not necessary, but it was a delightful ritual they had played each morning since their wedding. A tiny bit of formality just for the sake of honoring one another.

"Good morning, Mr. Darcy."

He held a chair for her, and she sat beside him.

"Mrs. Reynolds just sent in the chocolate pot. I knew you would soon follow."

He took the *molinet* between his palms, spun it briskly, and poured her a frothy cup of chocolate.

"Is it to your liking, madam?"

She sipped it. "Exactly, sir."

Mama never fancied indulging in chocolate, but it was Elizabeth's favorite luxury.

"The wind turned quite brisk last night. I thought to take the curricle with the hood today, unless you would prefer the coach."

How many choices daily life now entailed!

"I have rarely ridden in a curricle. I should like that."

"In the spring, I wish to teach you to drive. There is a low phaeton in the barn that has seen little use since my mother's passing. You might like it for traversing the estate."

"I am so accustomed to walking. It is still difficult to fathom a property I cannot cross comfortably on foot."

"It is quite possible we will require three days full to complete all the visits, even if we keep them to the customary quarter hour each."

"Surely you jest."

"My dear, you know I have not that capacity." His eyebrows rose.

That was not entirely true; he could be very amusing at times. But he had little ability for intentional jocularity.

"I had not realized the scope of our task." She clasped her hands and tightly laced her fingers.

He cradled her hands between his. "My dear, the tenants will be as delighted with you as Mrs. Reynolds and the rest of the staff. I have not encountered so many humming maids or smiling footmen in years. Mrs. Reynolds seems years younger. I have every confidence in you."

"Did I not tell you the same thing every time before we went out in London? I do not recall it affecting a great alteration in our spirits when I did."

He kissed her forehead. "You have no idea what difference it has made to me. No, I will never like being in company, but having you by my side changes everything."

"Now you are going to make me feel guilty … or misty-eyed" She dabbed at the corner of her eye with the back of her hand.

"Neither of those is my intention." He pushed his chair back. "Shall I have the curricle brought around?"

"Yes do, before my nerves resemble my mother's."

"Heaven forfend! Do not threaten me so!" He chuckled and left.

She drank down the last of the chocolate and hurried upstairs for her wraps and trusty notebook.

Elizabeth tucked a lap rug around herself against the morning's chill. Even with the calash in place, the curricle was far less warm than the coach. Darcy flipped the reins and the horses eased the curricle forward with fluid grace.

Papa was an indifferent horseman, at best. Not so her husband. He enjoyed an uncanny rapport with the beasts, one she had never witnessed before. Somehow he made driving look effortless. Perhaps he would succeed in teaching her what Papa could not.

"I thought to begin at the home farm. Mr. Steadman has managed it for many years. His wife is a steady woman, mother to three sons and a daughter. She is well acquainted with the estate and those on it."

"I imagine you could also recite the names of all their children and lineage of the all the farm's horses. Yet in London, you could not recall the names of half the guests at Bingley's party, despite having encountered them regularly in society."

"I remember what is significant."

She patted his shoulder and the lines around his eyes softened.

It would take him some time to become accustomed to being teased. But he was improving.

"Mrs. Steadman has run Pemberley's dame school for nearly ten years. She has seen to it that every child on the estate learns to read and write."

"I think I like her already."

"Mrs. Reynolds esteems her. In fact, it was she who facilitated the introduction resulting in the Steadman's marriage."

"Is Mrs. Reynolds in the habit of matchmaking?"

Darcy coughed. "Hardly. I know you do not know her well yet, but truly, can you see her spending her idle moments matching unsuspecting couples?"

"I do not imagine she has idle time in the first place. I am not entirely convinced that the dear woman ever sleeps."

"You are not the first to wonder." He pointed into the grey landscape. "There, you can see the farmhouse just beyond the rise. That is Thistledown."

An impressive farmhouse stood in the middle of a neat yard with a large garden plot just off what was probably the kitchen side.

Darcy stopped the curricle near the house. A boy ran up to take charge of the horses and Darcy helped her down.

A stout matron in a plain, serviceable cap and drab dress greeted them at the door. She had plump, rosy cheeks and walked with a soft rolling motion that must have lulled many a cranky baby to sleep. Just the sort of woman who belonged in a place named Thistledown.

"Good morning, Mr. Darcy," she curtsied, eyes on Elizabeth.

"May I present Mrs. Steadman?"

"Pleased to make your acquaintance, Mrs. Darcy. Come in, I will fetch the mister." She shuffled through the vestibule toward the back of the house.

She paused at a half-open door, knocking sharply. "Mr. Steadman, you are wanted in the parlor."

"Aye, missus." The voice was low and coarse as unhewn timber.

She continued on, and they followed.

The house was clean and tidy, that was no surprise. It seemed everything on Pemberley was. Touches of warmth and family waited at every turn: a bunch of dried flowers tucked atop a door frame; a tin soldier balanced on a chair rail; a book of stories, left open on a chair. A family did more than just reside in these walls. They lived here and made it home.

The parlor greeted them with warmth and as much comfort as faded furniture and well-used cushions could offer. A row of dear little stools sat before the fireplace, no doubt for children learning their letters.

"Pray sit down." Mrs. Steadman gestured toward the couch.

They sat and Mr. Steadman ambled in.

His coat was neat and his face and hair clean, but every inch of him cried 'farmer'. He carried a love of the land and instinctive understanding of it with him, bearing it like a family crest on a coach. No wonder Darcy trusted him with the home farm.

He pulled a chair close to Darcy and sat down.

They immediately launched into a discussion regarding the state of fields and livestock. The drainage on the east field was worrisome. Next season, they needed to consider adding a new bull for breeding stock.

Mrs. Steadman pulled a tall stool close to Elizabeth. "You won't get a word in edgewise when the Master and the mister get talking about the estate."

Perhaps not, but it was pleasing to see Darcy so animated in a conversation.

"I am told you teach the dame school."

"Indeed, I do. It came rather natural. When I was teaching my own youngsters, the other children were ever underfoot. You know how young ones is. So, I gathered them in and taught them, too. Next thing I know, they kept showing up expecting to learn, so I settled in to do it." She looked out the window.

The way her expression softened, she was probably seeing the faces of children she taught, now grown with children of their own.

"I expect you will be wanting to take that on now, as Lady Anne did?"

Elizabeth gasped and her jaw dropped. Mr. Steadman stopped talking and everyone gazed at her.

The Mistress of Pemberley probably should not be staring slack jawed, but there was little to be done for it

"Ah … I … no, I see no need, unless of course you find yourself weary of it. Clearly, the children's needs are being well met."

Mrs. Steadman's eyes lit. "I should very much like to continue on as I have been, madam."

"Then that is what shall be done. Pray send word if you need aught for your efforts."

Darcy blinked slowly at her—the equivalent of a vigorous nod in most men.

Mr. Steadman leaned back in his chair, arms folded comfortably over his chest. "When shall we expect the

Pemberley Ball, sir? Will you be using the traditional date, or picking another?"

Mrs. Steadman clucked her tongue. "The children began asking if they would be invited the moment they learned Pemberley was to have a new mistress."

Ball?

Darcy did not even blink. "We have not settled on all the details yet. Plans will be announced soon. Pray excuse us. We have many calls to pay today."

Elizabeth and Darcy rose.

"Perhaps when things are better settled, we might discuss the children over tea?" Elizabeth settled her wrap around her shoulders.

"I would fancy that very much, madam."

Darcy escorted her back to the curricle and helped her in. Bright sunshine had broken through the morning chill.

"You never mentioned a Pemberley Ball." She folded the lap rug and set it aside.

"I had not given it much thought until she mentioned it. Until Father's passing, we hosted a Christmastide Ball each year."

"Do you think it is widely expected one will be held this year?"

"I do not know, but, upon hearing Mrs. Steadman, I think it quite possible."

How could he say such a thing so calmly?

"I would not wish to be remembered for disappointing the entire village."

"Caroline Bingley hosted the ball at Netherfield with but a fortnight to plan. I do not see why we cannot. The traditional date for Pemberley's ball is the twenty eighth of December. Surely five weeks will be sufficient." He urged the horses into motion.

"My mother often hosted events at Longbourn, but she never organized a ball, much less one including children. I have no experience, no idea of what must be done."

"Mrs. Reynolds has records from every event ever given at Pemberley. Surely those will provide you with all the direction you should need to make it quite manageable."

Of course he considered it manageable. It was what one did with something they had never orchestrated themselves.

"Do you truly understand the magnitude of such an event?"

"I know Caroline Bingley accomplished it. You are far more capable than she. I would not suggest such a thing if I thought you destined to fail."

Of course he would not, yet …

"I suppose then, on December twenty eighth we shall have a ball. I shall speak to Mrs. Reynolds tonight."

After a full day of calls and a quiet dinner, Elizabeth asked Georgiana to join her in Mrs. Reynolds' office.

A cheery fire crackled in the little fireplace, warming the room to a cozy cheer. A neat stack of ledgers waited on the little table. Was it always piled with books?

Cook and Mrs. Reynolds rose and curtsied.

"I thought you might wish to hear Cook's suggestions as well, Mrs. Darcy." Mrs. Reynolds said.

"Of course. Thank you."

How foolish not to have thought of that herself.

Georgiana stared at her as though she expected Elizabeth to say something wise or witty. Neither was likely to occur.

"Mr. Darcy and I have decided to reinstate the traditional Pemberley Christmas Ball this year." Elizabeth lowered herself to the remaining chair. "As I understand, the event has not been held since his father's passing."

"Exactly so, madam." Mrs. Reynolds tapped the stack of ledgers. "These are the plans from the balls and the Pemberley receipt books, as well. Notes have been made on all the menus regarding the success of each dish and the guests' reactions, including the year a French chef was employed for the event."

Georgiana tittered and covered her mouth. "I think I remember that year. I was far too young to attend even the children's part of the ball, but I recall Father's muttering and complaining about the fracas the man chef caused in the kitchen."

"The Master did not see fit to continue his employ after the Christmastide season." Cook grumbled and shifted in her seat. "I believe it was Lady Matlock's suggestion he was hired in the first place."

Something about the way Mrs. Reynolds' lips wrinkled hinted that she had not approved the idea.

"Did Lady Matlock have considerable input into Pemberley events after the loss of Mrs. Darcy?"

"Oh yes, madam. She took it upon herself to oversee every last detail as if she were mistress herself. All her notes are here as well. You will see most clearly, her tastes were quite different to Lady Anne's."

"Aunt Matlock argued with my brother when he decided to cancel the ball." Georgiana bit her lip, wide-eyed and a little pale.

"She was not pleased with the Master's decision and tried vigorously to change his mind. One year, and only one year, he gave in to her persuasions."

Georgiana gasped. "I participated with the children that year. It was rather awful."

"Awful?" Elizabeth cocked her head and stared. "That is a very strong sentiment."

Cook huffed and crossed her meaty arms over her ample chest. It was rumored she could heft half a hog over her shoulder and butcher it with her cleaver in less than a quarter of an hour. Whilst that was likely an exaggeration, the scullery maids never talked back to her.

"We seldom speak of that year." Mrs. Reynolds looked aside. "The Master was laid up with a severe head cold. Lady Matlock took it upon herself to improve upon our traditional plans without disturbing his convalescence."

"She changed the menus," Georgiana whispered.

"Begging your pardon, Miss, and with all due respect to *her ladyship*," Cook leveled a firm gaze at Elizabeth, "the Lady meddled with things she did not understand. There is a way Pemberley does things. Our people expect things to be a certain way, foods to have particular flavors, served in a traditional way. When they are not, there is ... disappointment all around. And when disappointed people indulge in a great deal of punch ..."

"Or they are very young and unlearned at keeping opinions to themselves ..." Georgiana stared at her hands.

"The young Miss was left very distraught by the many complaints," Cook muttered something under her breath.

"What kind of complaints?"

Georgiana squirmed in her chair. How very sensitive to criticism she seemed.

"There were no gingernuts and the children were most disappointed. A new receipt was used for the shortbread, and she insisted on a different paste for the minced pies. I told her, I did, that our people would not like the changes. But the Lady insisted they should be grateful for what they were given." Cook pushed her glasses higher on her nose.

"I expect it had been many years since Lady Matlock had interacted with young ones. She did not plan well for their activities." Mrs. Reynolds shrugged.

"I do not think she planned at all! She insisted we should sit quietly and observe the dancing and the card playing, with little else to do but bemoan the lack of gingernuts." Georgiana dropped her chin into her palms with a huff.

"I see." Elizabeth ran her pencil along her lower lip. "Am I then to understand new additions to the celebrations are not welcome?"

"I would not say that, no not at all. It makes Pemberley sound a bit … backwards … and that is hardly the impression the Master would have us give you," Mrs. Reynolds said. "Tradition is indeed important. But that is not to say new things are unwelcome. Changes and additions are quite enjoyable when they do not take the place of what people love and anticipate. Disappointment sours an evening."

"I wonder … my mother never included children at a proper Christmas party. She thought it entirely unsuitable."

Mrs. Reynolds, Cook and Georgiana gasped.

"You do not wish to include the children?" Mrs. Reynolds' fingers tightened on the edge of the table.

"Oh, sister, you must forgive me for disagreeing, but I fear—"

"Pray, wait, you misunderstand. I would not want to disappoint the children. I do not suppose to exclude them. I was just considering—is the last Christmas Ball still well remembered?"

Mrs. Reynolds and Cook glanced at one another, an entire conversation passing between them in nods, raised eyebrows and creased foreheads.

"It is not something we commonly talk about," Cook said.

"But we must still choose not to talk about it, so perhaps it is still fresh in memory. Pemberley events rarely go awry ..." Mrs. Reynolds said.

"My concern is if we invite the children to the ball, we are inviting comparison to the previous event, already setting up talk and speculation. That cannot be a desirable thing."

"What have you in mind?" Georgiana pulled back a little and gazed at her through narrowed eyes.

"I thought to do something different for the children, something entirely new. If they and their parents can anticipate a special event, perhaps then they will be less apt to dwell upon the past."

"Something just for the children?" Mrs. Reynolds stroked her chin with her knuckle, eyes turned up toward the ceiling.

"A picnic on Christmas day. We might serve a cold supper on the lawn and have games for them to play: rounders, racing hoops, perhaps even a little archery, hoops and graces, buffy gruffy ..."

"Oh, the boys would like footraces as well," Georgiana said.

"We might make up plates and plates of biscuits, the children taking home with them what is not eaten here." One of cook's eyebrows rose while the other drew down over her eye, twitching slightly as though she were keeping count of something.

"Canopies may be erected in the garden, and tables and chairs to accommodate quite a number." Mrs. Reynolds sorted through the ledgers until she came to one with a faded blue cover. She flipped it open and scanned through pages.

"I know it will be additional work for the staff, especially considering the ball. Do you think it might be too much?"

Mrs. Reynolds turned to a blank page and pulled her pencil from behind her ear. Mumbling to herself, she scribbled down a list. She studied it a moment, turning her head this way and that.

"I think it entirely doable. Particularly if it means we do not host a family ball."

Elizabeth turned to Georgiana. "What do you think? Tell me honestly though. I should be very vexed to hear you say now that you like the notion only to discover in a month you hated the very mention of it."

"We have never held a Christmas picnic, but that does not mean it is not a good idea. I rather like it." Georgiana's tone did not match her words, but perhaps it was a start.

"I am pleased to hear you say so. Perhaps you might take on the running of it."

"Me!"

Did it hurt when her eyes bulged like that?

"Who better? Your memories of what you did not like will assist you to plan an event you would."

Mama had her and Jane assist in planning tea parties and other small events when they were far younger. It should not be too much for a girl of Georgiana's age to manage.

"I have never done such a thing before. I do not know."

"You must learn how at some point. What better event to begin with, especially with Mrs. Annesley to assist you."

Georgiana hunched and her brows drew together. Had it been Lydia, a tantrum would have immediately followed.

Had Georgiana never been asked to do anything before?

Mrs. Reynolds pulled another ledger from the stack and opened it. She handed it to Georgiana and pointed to the open page.

"Your lady mother held harvest picnics several times, always with the children included. Those are her notes. It should not be a difficult thing to start from those plans and adjust as we need."

Georgiana traced the neat scrolls of her mother's handwriting with her fingertip, her lips moving silently as she read. "With Mama's help, I think, perhaps, I can."

"Then it is a done thing. You shall plan the picnic instead of holding a family ball. How should we alter the menus, then?"

Mrs. Reynolds found the three most successful menus from previous balls and they scrutinized them long into the evening.

Elizabeth carried a candle and walked Georgiana to her room before retiring to her dressing room. The maid assigned to tend her appeared a moment later. How had she known? Perhaps Mrs. Reynolds sent word for her to be ready?

Darcy wanted to hire a proper French ladies' maid, but a French maid was for women of high society, true ladies, not country maids pretending to the office.

No, she should not think of herself thus. Darcy, Jane, Mama, even Mrs. Reynolds had told her often enough.

But they did not understand. Pemberley was not Longbourn; so many more people depended upon her and her decisions here.

And Christmastide gatherings? There were so many more people to please and so many different conflicting opinions of the roles of traditions and new ideas.

How was she to satisfy them all?

The maid helped her out of her gown and took down her hair, plaiting it into a thick braid.

"Will there be anything else, madam?"

Elizabeth shook her head and the girl disappeared through the silent servants' door.

Longbourn was not grand enough to have servants' stairs. They came and went along the same paths as the family, not nearly so separated as those who served here. Elizabeth still did not recognize some of the scullions and stable boys. How odd, living among strangers in one's own home.

Even now, as grand and lovely as it was, Pemberley still did not quite feel like home. She did not know every room, every passage as she did Longbourn. The stains on the upholstery and scars on the floorboards were not familiar friends, with stories to tell and reminisce of the days they had shared together. Everything was new and different, uncomfortable with her intrusions. As though getting to know her as much as she was trying to become acquainted with it.

New acquaintances were always difficult, especially in that period when one was not sure if they would become friends or just remain connections one acknowledged with a nod from across the street.

Despite all the people surrounding her, Pemberley was lonely.

She was not accustomed to being lonely.

She put out the candle and allowed her eyes to adjust to the moonlight. Just enough shone through the windows to allow her to make her way to the bedroom they shared.

Darcy snored softly, one arm thrown over his face, the other lay across her pillow.

She untied the belt of her dressing gown and slid under the counterpane. He shifted slightly, rolling toward her. She nestled her head into the hollow of his shoulder and his arm slid around her waist. Who would have thought this the way he would prefer to sleep?

All in all, she would rather have been able to talk, but when he slept so soundly, she could not bear to wake him. If she could not have his conversation, his warm presence around her provided a comforting consolation.

❧ Chapter 2

SUNBEAMS TEASED HER awake and alerted her that she was alone. That was not unusual, Darcy barely slept until dawn most mornings. He hated to rouse her as much as she him, so he rose quietly, and disappeared before she ever knew he had moved.

It was thoughtful and considerate to be sure. But the bed was large and empty, and the space beside her cold. There was a price to be paid for sharing a room and a bed with him. Most mornings, it was entirely worth it. But some days, the loneliness ached.

She rang for the maid and dressed. If he was not out riding, he would be in his study, preparing his correspondence before breakfast. He had invited her to join him several times, but since Mama met with

Hill first thing in the morning, it seemed the right time to meet with Mrs. Reynolds, too.

Perhaps not today, though.

She made her way down the grand staircase's wide marble steps. The broad expanse was beautiful, but it often reminded her how much she missed Longbourn's awkward, creaky stairs. The white and grey streaked stone did not creak or moan. It did not talk with her and acknowledge her passing, but only stood silent as a liveried servant doing its job.

The study door stood open a crack. An invitation? A welcome?

Hopefully, perhaps both. She scratched at the door and pressed it open.

Darcy hunched over his desk, peering at a document. Quill in hand, the nib hovered over a half-written sheet, covered in the precise loops and lines of his hand.

The room was neat and exact as he. The elegant mahogany and leather furniture had been chosen placed and placed for efficiency. Every book, every article had a place and resided there without argument. Even the sunbeams seemed to strike the desk in a precisely ordered way.

"Elizabeth?" He lay his pen aside and jumped to his feet. "What is wrong?"

She opened her mouth, but found no words to speak. She rushed into his warm arms and buried her face into his coat. The wool tickled her nose and scratched her cheek. It smelt like him, like acceptance and comfort, and she pressed in closer.

He cradled the back of her head with his hand and laid his cheek atop her head.

His words often failed, but his actions made his meaning clear.

"What is troubling you?"

She sniffled and shrugged. "I am not really sure."

"Pray do not tell me it is your nerves." He kissed her forehead.

She sniggered. "What, you do not wish to befriend them as my father has my mother's?"

"No."

He guided her to the window seat, the only place in the room where they might sit side by side. She leaned back against the window frame. The cool air around the glass soothed her raggedness.

"Did your interview with Mrs. Reynolds go poorly last night?"

"No, no, not at all. It went very well in fact. She produced all the plans from previous balls, giving us a grand start on planning this one. Georgiana even found her place to help."

"Indeed? I did not anticipate she would take on any such a responsibility. I am pleased she is willing. Pray, what is she to do?"

Elizabeth looked aside and chewed her knuckle. "She told us how little the children enjoyed the last ball. We decided to not to include the children this year. Rather, we will hold a Christmas picnic for them. I know it has not been done before and such a change may not be very welcome. I hope it does not displease—"

He took her shoulders in his hands and gripped her firmly. "Elizabeth, pray stop. You make it sound as though you expect me to be some ogre waiting to find fault with everything you do. Do you truly see me that way?"

"No, no, not at all."

"Have I not discussed with you the changes that I have initiated and those which I yet hope to implement?"

"At great length."

"Then you see. I am not averse to change."

"But Mrs. Reynolds—"

"She waxed on about Pemberley's traditions?"

Elizabeth nodded a bit more vigorously than she intended.

He leaned his head back and stared at the plaster-work moldings on the ceiling. "Oh my dearest, Mrs. Reynolds is a dear and wonderful woman for whom I have the deepest fondness and appreciation. All that is not to say she is without her foibles. Tradition happens to be one of those. She was very fond of both my parents. I think she remembers those days with perhaps more partiality than they rightfully deserve. Do not permit her nostalgia to prevent you from making your mark as Mistress of Pemberley. This is your home now, as much as it is mine."

A knot tightened in her throat so taut it brought tears to her eyes. She sniffled and swallowed it back.

"The Christmastide entertaining is yours. Do with it what you will, and it will be pleasing. I just pray you, no playing of characters drawn from a hat, and do not ask me to dance with any woman but you. With those two requests fulfilled, I am pleased with whatever you choose to do."

"I believe your desires may be accommodated, sir."

He smiled a smile that for the moment made her believe all would be right in the world.

Would that she might rest in his confidence as easily as he.

He made it all sound so simple, so obvious. Perhaps it had been silly to become so concerned over something so minor. Still, parties and balls were tricky beasts apt to turn on one like a cornered fox.

Once the season was over she could rest more easily.

A fortnight later, a letter appeared on his desk. An unwelcome letter. A letter he would have preferred to ignore.

He raked his hair and stormed out of his study.

The room was too confining, far too confining. He needed space to walk ... and to think. Had it not been raining, he would have been on horseback, galloping through a field until he and his horse were lathered and out of breath.

But why should the weather cooperate today when nothing else did?

The gallery—that was the place!

He took the steps of the grand staircase two at a time, leaving his heart racing and breath coming in hard pants.

That helped.

Cold radiated from the bright windows. He rubbed his hands together briskly. With no fire to chase the chill away, his Darcy and Fitzwilliam ancestors peered down from their portraits with frosty stares.

He paced the length of the gallery, twice, and came to a stop before Lord and Lady Matlock. Prickles raced along the back of his neck.

Why? Why?

They had a perfectly good townhouse ... in London. They liked to entertain ... in London. Their yearly twelfth night ball was anticipated among the *ton* ... in London. That was where they belonged for Christmastide ... in London.

What possessed Lady Matlock to decide to spend the holiday season in Derbyshire? At least she should have had the basic decency to keep to her own seat until invited otherwise.

The invitations for the ball were set to go out tomorrow. That should have kept them at home until the day before the ball. How was he going to tell Elizabeth that their arrival was imminent?

Clearly, he should never have answered the Matlocks' congratulations on their nuptials. He stalked away from the glowering Matlock portrait.

How could he ignore the backhanded slights made against his bride? Mother had warned him to control his Fitzwilliam temper. Allow the calmer, Darcy blood to temper the hot-headedness.

He should have listened.

No doubt his sharp words and challenge to Lady Matlock's insulting insinuations raised enough Fitzwilliam ire to fuel a war of wills. One he had no desire to wage, especially with Elizabeth in the middle.

Unfortunately, hindsight offered few answers. He required immediate, actionable answers before he was called upon to negotiate a truce not even His Majesty's emissaries would embark on lightly.

The back of his neck prickled as though he were being watching. He turned and stared out of the window.

No, that was simply not possible.

He ran to the window and pressed his forehead to the glass. Two coaches and a wagon trundled down the main lane toward Pemberley. The distance blurred the details, but there was little question the Matlock crest adorned both those carriages.

He tore down the stairs. Where would Elizabeth be this time of day? Mrs. Reynolds would know, but where would she be?

At the base of the stairs, where he nearly collided with her.

"Master?" She grabbed the banister.

He caught her elbows and held her until she regained her balance. "Forgive me. Pray, where is Mrs. Darcy?"

"She planned to call on tenants this morning, the east-most cottages as I recall."

"Should she not be at home to receive guests?"

"I do not believe she has established her at home days yet. Unexpected callers—"

"Are nearly at the door, Mrs. Reynolds." He glanced over his shoulder toward the front door.

"Pray excuse me, sir. I do not understand."

"The Matlock coaches approach as we speak. Two, with a wagon of luggage. I cannot image they are planning for a quarter hour's social call."

Mrs. Reynolds' eyes grew wide. "I shall have their rooms readied directly." She bit her lip. "Mrs. Darcy did not expect them. She intended to use the rooms the Earl and his family favor to accommodate her aunt and uncle later this month."

"The Gardiners are most reasonable people. I have no doubt they will be able to better weather a change in accommodation than my aunt and uncle."

A deep furrow shadowed her brow. "Yes, sir. Do you desire a tray of refreshments for them as well?"

"Yes, yes, that is an excellent plan. Send a footman in search of Mrs. Darcy. Instruct him to say we have guests, and her presence is required immediately."

She twitched her head in a little 'no' but said, "Yes sir," curtsied and hurried off.

Three quarters of an hour, perhaps a bit less. He had that long to prepare.

Pressing his temples, he retreated to his study. What were those things Aunt Matlock complained about most vehemently?

Food.

She wanted traditional Fitzwilliam dishes at the table.

And bed clothes!

How could he have forgotten? She required two down mattresses, one to sleep on and one to sleep under, and the bed ropes needed to be tightened. Oh, the counterpane? Which one did she demand? He rang for the butler and jotted notes for the cook.

Sampson appeared at the door. "Mrs. Reynolds sent—"

"Good, then you understand. Send the junior footmen to help the upstairs maid prepare the bed for Lady Matlock. One for Lord Matlock as well. He demanded the down mattresses replaced with flocked the last time they stayed." He shoved the hastily scrawled paper into Sampson's hand. "Give this to the cook. The menus must be changed for tonight's dinner— oh, and tell her they prefer to keep fashionable hours even in the country."

"Immediately, sir." Sampson bowed and disappeared.

What else? Surely he was forgetting something. No doubt Aunt Matlock would take great pleasure in reminding him.

"Brother?" Georgiana tiptoed in. "Is it true, what the maid just told me?"

"The Matlock coaches are on their way here? Yes, I saw them. I just received her letter this morning, but she did not say they would arrive today."

Georgiana blanched. He hurried to her side lest she swoon and fall.

"I do not wish to see them ... to see her."

He helped her to his favorite chair near the fire. The leather wingback engulfed her, making her look so like a little girl.

"She was so ..."

He crouched beside her. "I know she was not kind to you when you stayed with her after ..."

"You can say it, brother, after Ramsgate. Elizabeth has been so kind and gracious to me. She is so understanding. I had almost forgotten how terrible—" She pressed her fist to her mouth.

"I will not allow her—"

"Pray forgive me, brother, but how do you think you will stop her? No, she will take every opportunity she can find or manufacture to recap my failings, to criticize me, and to remind me how fortunate I am not to have been shipped off to Scotland for my deeds. Then she will lament how unfortunate it is that I am now related to *him*!" Her words tumbled out in a screech and she sprang to her feet.

"She has not." He gritted his teeth, hands clenched.

"Indeed she has." She ducked behind the chair. "Her last letter went on for pages about how it was entirely inappropriate for me to be connected to him. She said I should take every effort to carefully avoid the influence of my new sister—not the one married to *him*. Can you imagine? She declared Elizabeth must surely be a trial and a daily evil to be tolerated."

And that same woman expected to be a welcome guest in his house?

"Make no mistake, she comes with a purpose. She is determined to put both of us, Elizabeth and me, in our places. You must believe me, I am quite certain of it. If she has her way, I will soon be promised to a Scottish lord's youngest son and Elizabeth will be sent off for a long visit to your property in Scotland to chaperone me as I meet my future husband."

"Why did you not tell me?"

She looked away, chewing her knuckle. "It was … in her most recent letter to me … perhaps a se'nnight ago. I have been so dumbstruck by the shock of it all. How could I tell you something that would upset you so much? I did not envision we would see her again so very soon."

He rubbed his jaw. "Indeed not."

"Pray do not make me face her now, I simply cannot." Her eyes filled with tears.

"Go upstairs then and inform Mrs. Annesley you are not to be disturbed by any save Mrs. Darcy and that I shall personally sack her if she fails in this duty. You do not need to see Aunt Matlock tonight."

"Thank you, brother, thank you." She bounded away, a young doe fleeing from a poacher.

He sank into the empty chair.

How dare Aunt Matlock attempt to interfere in his family thus? His arms twitched and hands flexed, quivering. His boot heel bounced on the carpet, ready to leap.

If she were a man …

This would not do. Somehow he must get himself under better regulation before they arrived.

Elizabeth burst through the kitchen door, heart racing and gasping for breath. Mrs. Reynolds met her just a step inside.

"Thank heavens you are come, madam. We are in such an uproar."

"What happened?"

"The Earl of Matlock and his family, they have just arrived!"

"The Earl? I was told they were not in the country this time of year."

Surely this must be a humbug at her expense. But no, Mrs. Reynolds would never condone such a thing.

"I can only imagine they wish to honor your marriage with a Christmastide visit."

Perhaps it was wrong to consider it very little honor. More like an inspection.

"Cook is working on the new menus."

"Changes to the menu? Did Lady Matlock—"

"No, mum, it were Mr. Darcy who ordered them." Mrs. Reynolds pulled a paper from her apron pocket.

The handwriting was his, though written without his normal neat precision. "He countermanded nearly everything …"

"I know, madam." Mrs. Reynolds pressed her lips into a hard line, her brows rising just a mite.

So, he did not find her management of the menus sufficient. Would that he simply have told her.

"In the future, I suppose then he must approve the menus as well. We shall add that to the routine." Elizabeth forced a smile on her face, but it hurt.

"I am not sure it is necessary, I think—"

"No, it is necessary and precisely what we shall do." She squared her shoulders. "I will join our guests shortly, after I change clothes."

She strode from the kitchen in careful, measured steps.

At least she knew now, before they entertained on a grand scale, what he thought of her skills. This must be a good thing. He ensured the Darcy name would not be tarnished by … by … an inferior mistress.

Surely she could learn these skills, though. Come the new year, she would devote herself to Lady Anne's journals and records, and perhaps purchase a few household manuals. That should help.

At the top of the stairs, two footmen bearing a rolled mattress nearly knocked her over.

"Your pardon, Mistress." The taller of the two stammered.

"What are you doing?"

"Changing the mattresses in the guest rooms."

"Why did Mrs. Reynolds mention nothing of this to me?"

"The Master, he gave specific directions as to what must be done."

"In which rooms?" Elizabeth looked over her shoulder.

Maids hovered like bees around several opened doors.

"The gold suite."

Why would he change the mattresses in those rooms?

She turned on her heel and strode the long corridor to the gold suite. Within, several maids bustled about cleaning, polishing, and wrestling with the bed ropes.

"Why are you working on this room now?" Elizabeth asked no one in particular.

The upper maid ran to her and curtsied. "Begging your pardon, Mistress. The master ordered these rooms be prepared immediately for the Earl's party."

"I see. What other rooms have been assigned to his party?" She forced her voice flat and level.

Some things the servants did not need to know.

"I understand the blue suite near the end of the hall is being readied as well."

"Carry on. Provide me a list of all that has been done when you are finished."

"Yes, madam." She curtsied and rushed back to her work.

Elizabeth skirted the footmen with the mattress and made her way back to her own chambers with slow and purposed steps. This was why mama had taught her to walk like a lady.

She shut the door very softly and clicked the lock. The warm rays of sunshine pouring through the windowpane failed to penetrate the cold ache lodged in her chest.

Why?

The key dug painfully into her palm. When had she begun clutching it so hard?

He said he trusted her skills, that she would be sufficient as Mistress of Pemberley. But those were just words, empty words.

She staggered to the window seat and collapsed into its embrace. One of her old shawls, one not fine enough to be worn by the Mistress of Pemberley lay crumpled in the seat. She pulled it around her.

Fitting, it was just as unsuitable as she.

Why had he not told her? He could easily have discussed it with her, told her the required changes and allowed her to save face among the staff. But now they knew she was not to be trusted. Any order she issued would be scrutinized and questioned.

At least at Longbourn there had been respect. Papa never questioned Mama's orders within the house just as she never interfered with his management of the farms and estate.

It was probably too much to expect she would enjoy such respect here as well. She had married outside her own sphere. Now she was paying the price for her aspirations.

She would recover. She would study and learn and prove she was a worthy Mistress of Pemberley. Even if he did not believe she could do it.

She drew the shawl over her head like a hood and hid her face in her hands. A little humiliation would not kill her.

But it cut deeply enough to make her wonder.

Chapter 3

DARCY PACED THE PARLOR. The carriages were nearly at the front door.

Where was Elizabeth? She knew how to receive guests and make people feel welcome. What was taking her so long to return?

Sampson opened the door. "The Earl and Countess of Matlock, and Colonel Fitzwilliam."

Fitzwilliam was among them? At least he would have an ally in this campaign.

Aunt Matlock swept past Sampson and into the parlor. "How nice to see you have not redecorated. Your mother had such fine taste. It would be a shame to change that in any way."

How odd, Mother's simple tastes were something that she usually complained about. Aunt Matlock excelled in her ability to pack criticism into every compliment?

"It is lovely to see you, too, Aunt."

"I, for one, am happy to be enjoying Pemberley's hospitality again, redecorated or not." Fitzwilliam shouldered his way past Sampson and his mother and extended his hand.

Darcy shook it firmly. "I am pleased you are with us. How were your travels?"

"Horrid, simply horrid." Uncle hobbled in and fell into the nearest seat. "Traveling with gout is a terrible thing. Push a stool over here, must get this leg up."

Fitzwilliam retrieved a small stool from the opposite side of the room.

Matlock carefully lowered his foot upon it. "Could not bear the thought of traveling all the way to town like this."

"So naturally we thought of you … and your new wife." Aunt glanced at the door, her smiled strained.

"I only received your letter this morning. Do you not suppose it appropriate to offer a bit more notice of your coming?"

"It is St. Nicholas Day, nephew." Aunt Matlock tossed her head and strode to the window, her back to them.

"What significance is that?"

"Gentlemen!" She sniffed. "I should not have expected you to be attentive to such a thing. Surely your wife is aware."

"Aware of what?" Darcy stared at Fitzwilliam who dropped down on the couch and shrugged.

"Really, Darcy, you should ask her. I am certain she would be glad to tell you."

"I pray you do me the kindness of an answer."

"St. Nicholas day is the customary day for Christmastide house parties to begin. What other day would Mrs. Darcy expect to begin receiving guests?"

Elizabeth had never mentioned such a thing? Did she know?

Surely, she did. She had certainly been planning for guests.

And her relations offered the courtesy of announcing their plans to her in a timely fashion.

"So what are Pemberley's plans for entertaining this season?" She trailed her fingers along the window's mullions and glanced at her fingertips. With another sniff, she withdrew a handkerchief from her sleeve and wiped her fingers. "Coal dust."

"Invitations to the Christmastide ball are to be delivered today."

"Today? For a ball on December twenty-eighth? What are you thinking? That is not nearly enough time."

"It is three weeks in advance."

"A month, at least, is customary."

"I am certain it will not be an issue. We have not held one in so long—"

"That is not my fault." She swiped at a spot on the window glass with her handkerchief.

"No one said it was your fault."

No one said the ball had anything to do with her at all.

"There is a proper way to manage these things."

"I am sure they are being well managed. Georgiana is planning a children's picnic—"

"Picnic? In December? For the children? Are they not to be invited to the ball?"

"My wife thought it best to hold a separate event for them."

"Pemberley does not do it that way."

"This is my estate, and we can do exactly what we choose. If you wish to invite children to Matlock, then by all means, do so. I wish you well. Here, we shall do as the mistress sees fit."

Aunt Matlock turned slowly, very slowly, just as Mother had done when vexed. "This is not an auspicious beginning, Fitzwilliam, not at all."

Why must she say his name like that? The way she did when he was a small boy who fell into the stream playing with his older cousins. He resisted the urge to drop his gaze to the floor and scuff his toes on the carpet.

"Traditions exist for a reason. They bring order to life. They are foundation; they inform people of what to expect and how things will be. You bring uncertainty and doubt when you attempt to change them. Only an upstart would undermine the foundations of an honorable family thus."

"Upstart?" Darcy's jaw fell open.

Had she really just said those words, in his home?

The door swung open, and Elizabeth slipped inside.

Her dress bore no road dust, and she wore slippers, not her half-boots. She must have changed since she arrived. Probably for the best.

Still, he would rather have had her at his side sooner.

He went to her, hand extended, but she pulled back as he approached. He started. Perhaps she did not wish to appear so familiar before his family.

Of course. She was right.

"Mrs. Darcy, I am glad you are come."

"I am sorry I was not here to greet you myself." She curtsied deeply enough to please the king.

The motion though was stiff and utterly unlike her. Was she as unsettled as he?

Fitzwilliam rose. "It is a pleasure to see you again, Elizabeth. Out walking the grounds? Pemberley is a lovely place for a ramble."

"I was calling upon the cottages on the east side of the estate and discovered a rash of sore throats. I must call for the apothecary."

Aunt's eyebrows climbed high on her forehead. "How good of you to be so concerned when you have so very much to do."

"I do not find it too much to manage."

"No doubt you are so eager because you called on your father's tenants regularly." Aunt turned up her nose and sniffed. "You may find the population of Pemberley a mite more challenging to oversee."

"Thank you for your concern, Lady Matlock."

If Elizabeth's voice became any more brittle, her words would surely shatter upon the floor.

"With all your new duties, do you still walk in the mornings?" Fitzwilliam stood between his mother and Elizabeth.

"Whenever I can."

"Perhaps some morning I might show you the spot where, in his boyhood, your dignified husband fell into the stream."

Aunt Matlock rounded on him. "My dear boy, you cannot monopolize her time that way. Her mornings are no doubt taken up with meeting with the house-keeper and attending her correspondence. I heard you were sending out invitations today."

Elizabeth's neck tensed. How tightly was she clenching her teeth?

"I will have yours delivered to your rooms." She glanced at Darcy with an expression he had never seen before.

One he would rather not see again.

"That would be most appreciated. How are your plans for the ball progressing?"

Elizabeth drew a deep breath and let it out very slowly. "Very well, thank you. With Mrs. Reynolds' excellent assistance, I am quite comfortable with our progress."

"Have you ever planned an event like this one?"

"My father was the principle land owner in our area. I am familiar with what is expected."

"Pray do not be offended, my dear. I am well aware your father is a gentleman. It is, though, a matter of scale. As I understand his estate was rather ... smaller ... than Pemberley."

"I am quite familiar with what is expected for an event of this magnitude."

"I should be very happy to help you in any way I can. Perhaps I should go over the menus—"

Elizabeth shot him another one of those expressions, more pointed than the last.

He ran a finger around the inside of his collar.

"—just to help ensure they will match the expectations of this region. Perhaps you do not know, but I was responsible for the last Pemberley Ball held on the estate."

"Georgiana had mentioned it. You do not need to trouble yourself, Lady Matlock."

"It will be no trouble at all. I should be very glad to lend my expertise."

All eyes turned to Darcy.

Uncle Matlock and Fitzwilliam seemed vaguely amused, but Aunt Matlock and Elizabeth were serious as death itself.

"What do you think nephew?"

"I believe the purview of planning social affairs is on the mistress of the house."

"And you would be entirely right. But a wise person, a wise woman, knows when it is appropriate to seek assistance." Aunt Matlock drew herself up very straight.

"I have sought assistance. Mrs. Reynolds has served the household through many such events."

"And I am certain she is a master of what must go on below stairs and behind the servants' door. I do not by any means belittle her expertise. She is truly a gem and has kept Pemberley running since the passing of my dear sister. But how would she know of the newest fashions in food or decoration?"

Darcy took a half-step forward. "Did you not just lecture me that tradition was more important than fashion?"

"As I understand, you are changing tradition by not having children at the Christmas Family Ball."

"I gather you do not approve." Elizabeth clasped her hands tightly before her.

"It is not for me to approve or disapprove, Mrs. Darcy. I was merely noting that traditions do not seem so significant to either of you after all. So again, I ask, shall I help you with your menus?"

"Since I am the newcomer here, perhaps I should leave that decision to my husband who apprehends so much of what is required to manage the estate. Pray inform me when you choose. Excuse me now, Mrs. Reynolds requires my attention." She curtsied and darted out before anyone could comment.

"She is a sensitive flighty little thing. So proud. I dare say she is most easily offended. She will not do well among the *ton*." Aunt tossed her head and turned back to the window.

Mrs. Reynolds entered, with a maid following close behind, bearing a tray of sandwiches and other dainties.

"Pray, refresh yourselves. Your normal rooms are prepared for you, and your things have been sent there. Pray excuse me." Darcy bowed his head and followed Mrs. Reynolds out.

Elizabeth had told a falsehood. She had no intention of going to Mrs. Reynolds. The poor woman was already at her wits' end with all the changes and needed no further disruptions. Elizabeth stormed up to the small sitting room near her chambers and shut her door.

That woman! She might be the wife of an earl and her husband's aunt, but the audacity! How dare Lady Matlock come in and cast such aspersions on her!

Elizabeth paced the length of the room like an unbroken filly anxious for release from her paddock.

She paused at the window and gulped breathes breaths of cooler air.

Perhaps though, just perhaps, Lady Matlock was right. What did Elizabeth know of high society and its expectations?

Still though, this was the country, not London. The guests for the Christmas ball did not mingle with the height of London society, Almack's Patronesses or the nobility. Except, of course, for the Earl and his family. The rest were comfortable country gentry, with a few knights and a baronet as well. No one would expect the heights of London fashion.

Would they?

She pressed her temples and sought the chair near the fireplace, a worn blue velvet chair Darcy's mother preferred. The chair's arms cradled her. At least something in this place welcomed her.

The door creaked open and Mrs. Reynolds appeared with her favorite tea cup, brought from Longbourn, and two tiny tea sandwiches.

"Do you fancy some refreshment, madam?"

No, she did not, not at all. Food sounded decided-ly unappealing. But Mrs. Reynolds looked so hopeful.

"Thank you."

Mrs. Reynolds placed the tray on the nearby table. "Are you well, Mistress?"

Elizabeth shook her head. It probably was unto-ward to make such an admission to a servant. Somehow Mrs. Reynolds' dark eyes required truth.

"How might I help?"

"I do not know. It seems we have guests among us now whom I have no idea how to satisfy."

"May I speak frankly, Mrs. Darcy?"

Elizabeth peered into Mrs. Reynolds' face. "I rely upon you to always be frank with me."

"It is unlikely you will be able to please them, no matter what you do."

Elizabeth started.

"Do not take offense, madam. It is their nature. Nothing and no one gives them pleasure. Their visits unsettled Lady Anne as well. She dreaded their com-ing with a fire hard to describe. She and Lady Matlock did not get on very well, you see."

"I had no idea."

"Few did. They kept their peace in company, but in private, well that was another thing altogether. I walked in on a few of their conversations and would be happy never to have done so."

"I had no idea."

"I do not believe the Master does either. Just know, nothing pleases Lady Matlock save having her own way. Even when she gets it, she is still likely to complain."

"How encouraging."

"Perhaps, but there is little point in fighting a battle you cannot win."

She pressed her knuckle to her lips.

So there it was. No matter what she did, she would fail.

"You may wish to look in on Miss Georgiana this morning. She is in her room. Mrs. Annesley says no one but you is to see her."

"Has she taken ill?"

"You might say she is taken with Matlock fever."

Elizabeth snickered. Oh, how she needed that levity, irreverent as it was.

"I will see to her after my tea."

Mrs. Reynolds curtsied and left.

She cradled her teacup in her hands and stared into the amber liquid.

How was she to comfort Georgiana when she had no idea of how to comfort herself?

The tea was barely warm, but sweet. Mrs. Reynolds had made her favorite blend and sweetened it just right. So efficient despite her mistress's failures.

The bite of sandwich was hard to swallow for the lump in her throat.

She set the tea things aside and steeled herself for another disappointment.

Georgiana's door was closed and doubtless locked as well. Lady Matlock was probably not one to respect a closed door. Elizabeth rapped softly.

A maid opened the door a sliver and peeked out. She nodded, a little relief in her eyes, and admitted Elizabeth.

Georgiana watched from the window seat, peeking from under a drab wool shawl; a dormouse hiding from a cat.

Mrs. Annesley sat nearby, sewing in the bright morning sun. Her mouth was drawn up, tight as her stitches, puckered a little at the sides.

"Have you seen her yet?" Georgiana waved at the maid to close the door.

The lock clicked softly.

"I just left them in the parlor downstairs."

"Why are they here?"

Mrs. Annesley's cheek twitched.

"The Earl's gout keeps them from London."

"So they come here to torment us instead? Oh it is not fair, not at all." Georgiana hid her face in the shawl's generous folds.

"What would you have us to do? We cannot simply turn them out."

"Why not?"

Mrs. Annesley's eyes bulged as she flashed a glare at Georgiana.

Elizabeth sat beside her. "It is an entertaining thought."

"Yes it is. I should insist my brother consider it."

Mrs. Annesley squeezed her temples.

Gracious, Georgiana looked very serious about the notion. Had she no understanding of humor?

Elizabeth would have to be very careful how she spoke to her.

"Colonel Fitzwilliam—Richard—is with them as well."

"He may stay. He is nothing like his mother."

"I am sure he will appreciate your verdict."

"The Christmas picnic cannot go on, can it?" Georgiana peeked over the edge of the shawl. "She does not approve, I am sure."

"All our plans are suspect to her. She demands the right to examine the menus for the ball."

"I cannot do it." Georgiana huddled in the corner of the window seat, as far away from Elizabeth as possible.

Was this how Georgiana usually responded to distress? The display bordered on Lydia's artifice.

"I cannot plan anything, not with her here. She will give me no rest until I capitulate to her will and give her control of everything. Pray do not ask me to."

"What are you not telling me? You are far too troubled for it to be about a mere picnic."

Georgiana pressed her fist to her mouth. "She has not forgiven me. She will never forgive me for ... for ... Ramsgate. She thinks I am entirely ruined ... she wants to send me away. She said so in her last letter."

"Your brother will not permit it."

She peeked through her fingers. "I know ... I know ... that is why I am here in my rooms. He said I might say up here whilst they are visiting. He ... he said I do not have to plan—"

"I see. Then your situation is well in hand." Elizabeth rose and turned away, fists clenched at her side.

"You are angry with me."

"Not at all. I simply better understand the workings of Pemberley and my place in them."

"Pray do not be angry with me, too."

"Your brother will see you are well taken care of." Elizabeth's voice broke, and she fled the room.

Mrs. Annesley follower her out. "Pray, Mrs. Darcy."

Elizabeth forced her feet to stop.

"What are your instructions, madam?" Mrs. Annesley peered up at her.

Hunched over just a bit, and short-sighted, her face wrinkled up as she stared. Her mouth, though, suggested much stronger feelings than her tone implied.

"My instructions?"

"Regarding Miss Darcy."

"It seems Mr. Darcy has given all the direction necessary."

"He has never spoken them to me, madam." She cocked her head just so, like one of the sitting hens at Longbourn used to do.

"Nor to me, either. Miss Darcy seems to understand his wishes quite clearly, though."

"And you wish me to—"

"Follow his instruction." Elizabeth's voice wavered on the final word.

"Very good, madam." Mrs. Annesley curtsied and trundled away.

Thank Providence; her own chambers were not far. Elizabeth ducked inside and locked the door.

Darcy had cancelled the plans for the picnic. He said he supported the notion, even sounded pleased that they were to try something new. Why had he said something he clearly did not mean?

Moreover, he saw fit to direct his sister's behavior. Having four sisters of her own was not enough to make her sufficiently knowledgeable to manage even that.

She was Mistress of Pemberley in name only.

Heavens above!

She pressed her back against the wall and slid to the floor. Lady Catherine prophesied this would be the result if she became Darcy's wife. The shades of Pemberley were being polluted by Elizabeth's presence. She was a stain, an embarrassment to him. What else could he do but cover for her failings and create the illusion of a competent mistress to those who might observe.

She wrapped her arms around her shoulders and clung tightly to the little composure she retained. Lydia, Kitty, even Mary at times, they were the silly girls who brought blushes and mortification to the family. Not her, she had always been a credit to her father, to her mother.

Now all that was gone.

All she had left was to play the role of hostess and allow Darcy to manage things as he saw fit.

Two steps down the hall, Fitzwilliam intercepted Darcy. "We need to talk."

Darcy grunted and waved him toward the study. Conversation held little appeal

Brandy.

That was his only chance at civility.

"A bit early in the day for this, is it not?" Fitzwilliam lifted the glass toward him.

Darcy swallowed a large gulp and chased it with a deep breath. "Your arrival warrants celebration."

"I argued against an unannounced visit."

"I will keep that in mind."

"I am on your side." Fitzwilliam fell into a chair near the fireplace and balanced his glass on his knee. "You are aware my mother has an agenda."

"Georgiana mentioned something about that last night."

"I cannot fathom why she is so bent upon managing Pemberley's ball. One would think she would be happy for a respite from all that work."

"She doubts Elizabeth's abilities."

"The patched up business with Wickham and her sister has rather poisoned Mother's opinion of her family."

Darcy growled under his breath and refilled their glasses.

"Wickham was taking revenge on me."

"Be that as it may, you are now brother to him." Fitzwilliam stretched out his legs and crossed his ankles.

"Do not remind me."

"Mother will, unceasingly."

"She would not dare."

Fitzwilliam sipped his drink and lifted his glass as if to toast.

"I will not permit it."

"You cannot stop it. You know she speaks her mind."

"A Fitzwilliam family trait." Darcy set his glass down hard on his desk. "I think her unexpected arrival has already upset my wife."

"You think so? You only think that the case? Truly, you amaze me."

"What do you want of me? Have you a suggestion how to manage this campaign, oh colonel of His Majesty's army."

"That is the problem. My mother is an expert in managing the wars of society. She specializes in subterfuge, not something to your or my tastes. Elizabeth is a new recruit in this conflict, one who may easily become a casualty."

"I will not permit it."

"I know you mean well, but that might be more difficult than you expect."

Dinner was served at the fashionable hour of eight.

Darcy's stomach grumbled and his temper matched. Dash it all, what a foolish time to eat. Why had he insisted they change plans to meet the Matlock's expectations? This was his home after all.

Was it not what a proper host did? Surely it is what Elizabeth would have done. She would approve of his order. Surely she would.

Why then had she only appeared in the drawing room to announce dinner, and not a moment before? She murmured something about a head ache, but refused to explain any further. Hopefully they would be able to talk tonight, in the privacy of their own chambers.

"I am surprised Georgiana is not with us." Aunt Matlock flipped open the napkin and tucked it in her lap.

"She is feeling poorly tonight," Elizabeth said softly, eyes cast down on her plate.

"Do you not worry about being too indulgent with her? She is becoming demanding and petulant. She declined to admit me when I tried to see her earlier this evening."

Darcy shrugged and glanced at Elizabeth, but she would not meet his gaze.

"She is a young girl. I see little harm in her not attending dinner one night," Darcy said.

"Forgive me, Darcy, but what know you of the management of young women?"

Aunt Matlock smiled at him so condescendingly, he nearly dropped his glass.

"I should think by now you would have turned over her management to someone who would know better. Do you not employ a companion for her?"

"We do, but Elizabeth—"

"The mistress of the house should not be burdened with such a task."

"She has four sisters. I should think she knows a great deal about the management of young ladies," Fitzwilliam raised his glass toward Elizabeth.

Lady Matlock laughed bitterly, "I suppose that experience would count for something. Still, Georgiana should have some sort of proper finishing."

"She does not desire to be sent off, anywhere," Darcy said. "I see no need to oppose her."

"Any other accomplishments she requires, Elizabeth can teach her or a tutor may be hired," Fitzwilliam said.

"One cannot hire a tutor for every accomplishment."

Elizabeth dropped her fork on her plate. The clink resounded through the room like the chime of a gong.

"Pray forgive me," she muttered into her plate.

Ordinarily she would have laughed and made fun at such a misstep.

Darcy called upon every ounce of self-control not to ask what the matter was.

"The carrot soup was excellent tonight," Fitzwilliam sipped the last of the soup from his spoon. "Pray is it a receipt you brought from Longbourn?"

No, the Longbourn soup was far superior to this sweet orange mess.

"Mr. Darcy specifically requested it tonight, from Pemberley's receipt books." Elizabeth glanced at him only briefly.

Pray that she not do so again! Her gaze was as sharp as a poacher's arrow.

"Do you not recognize it? It is an old Fitzwilliam recipe," Aunt Matlock dabbed her lips with her napkin. "It is quite delightful, is it not? The best carrot soup I have known."

Darcy would rather not have indulged in so many Fitzwilliam family recipes, but at least it kept Aunt Matlock's dinnertime complaints at bay.

"Be that as it may, I need more wine." Uncle Matlock tapped his glass with his fork.

A footman hopped into action and filled his glass.

Elizabeth rang the bell for the second course.

He tried to catch her gaze, but she turned aside. Was she intentionally ignoring him?

Small talk, tense and painful, made an unwelcome garnish for what should have otherwise been a pleasant meal. Throughout, he could not pry more than single word answers from Elizabeth, and she never looked at him.

The sweet course came, and with it the opportunity for the ladies to withdraw alone.

Elizabeth and Aunt Matlock alone together in the drawing room? Heaven forfend!

He rose. "Shall we proceed to the drawing room?"

Elizabeth turned very pale and trembled. Had Aunt Matlock disconcerted her so badly?

He had been right not to chance leaving her to his Aunt's predations.

Fitzwilliam offered Elizabeth his arm and escorted her to the drawing room, every inch a proper, somber officer. How did she manage to draw such correct behavior from him when no one else could?

"Will you play for us, Mrs. Darcy?" Aunt Matlock asked.

Darcy cringed and glanced at Elizabeth, but she stiffened and turned aside. He drew a breath to protest.

Aunt Matlock would be no kinder to Elizabeth than Aunt Catherine. Insisting the lady must practice more—indeed! The back of his neck twitched.

Elizabeth arranged some music and the first notes rang from the keyboard.

She gazed off into the distance. Usually when she sang, she looked at him. It was a special intimacy they shared; one others should not be privy to.

They must share the same mind.

Had she any idea of how beautiful she was?

From the corner of his eye, he caught Aunt Matlock's censorious glare. He was staring.

He averted his eyes, grumbling under his breath. Should not a man be able to look at what he pleased in the privacy of his own home?

Uncle called for a hand of cards, but insisted on whist. Aunt and Fitzwilliam immediately attended him.

"Here, Darcy, we need a fourth." Uncle Matlock waved him toward the table. His best commanding peer voice booming over Elizabeth's music.

Elizabeth did not particularly like whist, but still, it was rude of them to select something that would necessarily leave one and only one of the company out. He stood in the middle of the room, wavering between the pianoforte and the whist table.

"Pray excuse me. I have taken a headache." Elizabeth removed herself from the room.

Darcy took a step toward the door.

"Leave her go." Aunt flicked her fan open and fluttered it before her face. "She does not need you to nursemaid her. She has her maid for that."

He should go to her. This was utterly unlike her.

Yet, more than once he had been told that he was too protective, too controlling. Perhaps that was what was troubling her, and going after her would only make things worse.

He turned to the whist table and sat down, clenching his hand beneath the table.

Elizabeth ran upstairs, stumbling as she went. The unforgiving marble bruised her shin.

Somehow it fit. Even the house itself had turned against her.

She slowed and grasped the banister. How many times had Mama admonished her to walk like a lady? Apparently she had been correct.

The throbbing in her shin eased by the time she reached the dressing room she and Darcy shared. Her maid was there, waiting.

How did she know? Pemberley's walls must have eyes and ears, for she was always available when Elizabeth needed her.

She helped Elizabeth undress, and then slipped out of the servants' door, leaving Elizabeth alone.

Very, very alone.

For a few short weeks, Pemberley had seemed bright and welcoming to her.

How wrong she had been.

All those nagging voices in the back of her mind; the ones warning her she might not be up to the task; the ones she had silenced in her arrogance—they were entirely correct.

He did not even trust her to conduct drawing room conversation without his supervision. His relations effectively declared her too inferior to share a card table with them.

She threw open her chamber door, and stared into the bedroom they did not use.

From their first day at Pemberley, they had shared his bed chamber. But she could not go in there, not tonight.

She locked the door behind her and fell headlong onto the bed. The room was cold. The servants had stopped lighting the fire when it was clear it would not be used.

Fitting.

She could call a girl to light the fire easily enough, but to what point? Fire would do nothing to chase the chill lodged deep within.

Nothing would.

She would become accustomed to it, somehow. With study, and application, and effort she would master her role as Mrs. Darcy, just as she had chess when her father had insisted she learn. That had been challenging, but now she regularly bested him. She would do the same here.

At the very least, she would no longer be a source of embarrassment to him. Regardless, she would not permit Lady Catherine's pronouncements over her to be prophetic.

For tonight though, nothing remained to do. She climbed under the counterpane and one of the feather mattresses. Tomorrow she would instruct the maids to light the fire in this room.

Darcy dragged himself upstairs. What a stupid way to pass time. One rubber of whist was acceptable, but … how many? He had lost count. Whatever the number, it was utter foolishness and would not be repeated.

He had lost the last several few hands. His distracted play irritated even Fitzwilliam. How could he concentrate on something as trivial as cards when worrying for Elizabeth? At least now, he could see her, speak to her, and lay all that to rest.

The dressing room was empty.

Of course, she would have gone to bed by now. It was foolishly late.

He undressed without his valet. His state of mind would not tolerate the man's presence, no matter how quick and efficient he was.

His bedchamber door stood barely ajar. All the better, the sound of the door handle would not disturb her. He slipped in and paused, allowing his eyes to adjust.

The bed … it was empty, the bedclothes undisturbed.

Ice flowed through his veins.

Where was she?

He dashed back into the dressing room. The crystal knob to the mistress' chambers glinted in the moonlight.

Why would she be there?

He tried the door.

Locked.

The door was locked.

He staggered to a stool near his dressing table.

Why?

Perhaps it was a mistake.

In her weariness, had she locked this door instead of the one to the hall? She was not accustomed to that room, so she could have become confused, especially with a headache.

Why sleep there? Did she worry about keeping him awake if she could not sleep? It was like her to be so considerate, but unnecessary. If she was unwell, he wanted to be with her.

He paced the narrow moonbeam painting the floor.

Perhaps his aunt had distressed her more than he realized. Certainly that could cause her to retreat.

When he was upset, sometimes, at least before he had been married, he preferred to retreat in solitude.

Certainly, she needed time and a little solitude to work it all out. Tomorrow, no doubt, she would be to rights again.

Tomorrow.

He shuffled back to his bedchamber. A low fire glowed in the fireplace, filling the room with gentle warmth.

He pulled the cold sheets and counterpane around him, shivering without a warm companion to fill his arms. He closed his eyes, but did not sleep.

She rose before dawn the next day and rang for her maid.

"I will dress in this room today. I do not wish the master disturbed." Shivering, Elizabeth tied her dressing robe around her. "And have a fire lit here going forward."

"Yes, madam."

To her credit, the maid offered no expression whatsoever. She went about her job with perfect efficiency, preparing her mistress for another day.

A day filled with further opportunity for failure.

Elizabeth went downstairs. She pulled her shawl around her more tightly and ducked into the kitchen. How much warmer it was near the hearth fires.

Cook and her minions bustled about.

"Mrs. Darcy?" Mrs. Reynolds appeared at her elbow, eyes wide.

Elizabeth jumped. Longbourn's kitchen had never been surprised to see her.

"Is there something wrong?"

"No, no, not at all."

Surely the woman was perceptive enough to know Elizabeth was lying.

"Perhaps, you would like some tea, madam?"

"That would be lovely."

Mrs. Reynolds waved her hand. The footmen sitting at the table near the fireplace jumped up and offered her their chairs. They beat a hasty retreat.

She sat in the nearest one.

The kitchen was usually such a friendly homey place, not one where people ran from her.

"Do you wish to go over household matters now?" Mrs. Reynolds placed a teacup and a slice of toast before her.

"An excellent notion. Perhaps beforehand, though, do you know if Mrs. Annesley has any books on etiquette and entertaining, housekeeping manuals of any kind? Something perhaps not too old—"

"Ones reflecting recent fashions?"

"Yes, exactly."

"Indeed she does. She relies on them to instruct Miss Darcy. I expect you would like to review what she is being taught?"

Bless her discretion!

"Yes, yes, precisely."

"I will see those books sent to you directly."

"Have them brought to your office rather than to my chambers."

Her eyebrows rose, questions dancing in her eyes. "As you wish, madam." She hurried away.

Mrs. Reynolds never went anywhere slowly. She was always bustling about this way and that, much like Hill back at home.

Home.

She swallowed hard, but the lump in her throat did not subside. Why now to be so sentimental? Though she had been attached to Longbourn, leaving it had not been so very difficult.

Not as difficult as the look on Darcy's face last night.

She covered her eyes with her hand and squeezed her temples.

"Headache, madam?"

When had Mrs. Reynolds returned?

"Just a bit."

"May I fix you the tea I used to make for Lady Anne?"

Elizabeth nodded and several minutes later a fresh cup appeared before her.

Oh, but it was bitter.

She added sugar, then a little more. Surely it contained willow bark to be so pungent. The sweetening helped, and she drank it down.

"Perhaps now we might look over the needs of the house."

Mrs. Reynolds already had the housekeeping ledgers stacked nearby. "Concerning the menus …"

Her stomach wrenched. "Yes, as to those."

"We have made the changes requested by the master, but some of his requests we cannot accommodate. Green goose, mackerel and peaches are out of season and simply cannot be obtained."

"We must do the best we are able. Substitute what you must. There is no other thing for it. I will explain to him the limitations of season. Has it been his habit to place such requests?"

"No, madam. More commonly, when the Earl and his family arrive, his man brings their requests direct to us. We accommodate those demands as best we can."

Demands, an interesting choice of words.

Did Darcy think she would deny the requests of Pemberley's guests?

"If I may be so bold, madam, I believe they make the master uncomfortable when they visit."

"They make me uncomfortable." Elizabeth bit her lip.

She probably should not have said that.

Hill had been like part of the family—she was in fact a distant Bennet cousin, widowed young and established at Longbourn as no other relation had a place for her. Mama had never been as discreet with her as she should have been.

One more lesson Elizabeth needed to learn.

"Do you wish to pay calls on the estate today?"

Brilliant woman!

Did she realize how useful she was being or was she just stumbling upon the right things to say?

No, this was not by chance at all. She understood. Bless her.

"Yes. Just because we have company, it does not mean I should neglect my duties. Are you aware of visits which must be made?"

Mrs. Reynolds reached into her apron pocket. "I have a few notes …"

Indeed she did. One cottager's mother was in the final throes of consumption and would not likely see Christmas this year.

Elizabeth would visit them first. Aunt Gardiner said there was nothing like calling upon those with real tragedy to put your own little complaints in perspective.

Chapter 4

ONCE BEGUN, HER NEW routine continued, largely on its own momentum. She rose early, studied the books in Mrs. Reynolds office, met with her concerning the household, and left for her morning business.

Elizabeth would briefly greet her guests in the afternoon before departing to dress for dinner. Behind her closed and locked door, she would prepare for the horrid affair.

At dinner, she would endure Lady Matlock's comments and observations. On particularly good evenings, Fitzwilliam would regale them with stories from his deployments on the continent. In all likelihood, he carefully chose tales to be pleasing to the ladies. The shadows in his eyes suggested many more that he did not tell.

Georgiana remained hidden in her rooms, avoiding her aunt and her responsibilities.

Perhaps Lady Matlock had been correct after all in calling Georgiana petulant.

Agreeing with Lady Matlock? What was she thinking?

She rubbed her eyes with thumb and forefinger. Truly, Georgiana's behavior was too much, but if Elizabeth dared interfere, no doubt Darcy would see fit to overrule her again. Her heart could not withstand another such blow, so she kept her peace.

Darcy seemed sanguine enough about Georgiana's behavior. He said little regarding the menus once she explained the issues of availability. He and Fitzwilliam rode the estate during the day, and insisted the gentlemen and ladies adjourn to the drawing room together after dinner.

There, she would play and sing for them, nod at the stilted conversation, and excuse herself before anyone else retired. Though there was a fire in her chambers, the rooms were still cold. That would probably never change.

One night, Darcy followed just a few minutes behind her. He tried the doorknob, but the door was already locked. He knocked and called for her, but what was there to say? He desisted after a few minutes.

Some mornings later, the rain began as Elizabeth sipped her tea and grew more determined during her meeting with Mrs. Reynolds. It slapped the window glass in short, hard bursts, exercising its temper on the barrier.

She could not go out until it abated. Perhaps she might take up Georgiana's habit and keep to her own rooms today. She slipped out of the kitchen and past the morning room.

"Elizabeth!"

Lady Matlock's sharp screech sent shivers down her spine. She stopped.

Damn her feet.

"Do come in and join us this morning. You must keep company with us. We have seen so little of you recently."

A lady did not sigh, at least not where anyone could see her do so, no matter how powerful the urge.

Elizabeth turned and trudged into the morning room.

Richard rose and held out a chair for her, his expression vaguely apologetic.

Lady Matlock sipped her tea, peering over the rim of the cup. "You look well this morning. I feared you had taken ill."

"Thank you for your concern, madam. You will forgive me. I have been so busy—"

"Yes, yes, regarding that. It is high time we discuss plans."

"Have you something you wish to do whilst here?"

"Plans for your ball, you silly girl." Lady Matlock patted the table.

"Has Mr. Darcy expressed—"

"Absolutely nothing. What does he have to say in the matter? Such things are not the purview of men." She flipped her hand toward Richard.

He shook his head and rolled his eyes, his face a picture of tolerance and good humor. If only she could endure as he. But then, what was Lady Matlock to Napoleon?

"Pemberley's first ball in years is just three weeks away, and I have yet to review any of your plans. Georgiana has hardly left her room. Was she not to plan that ridiculous picnic for the children? Has anything been accomplished toward that end?"

"You have no reason for concern, Lady Matlock. I have everything well in hand."

Had Darcy not informed her he canceled the event?

"You see, Mother, it is exactly as I told you." Richard leaned forward and wagged his finger toward her. "Elizabeth has matters well in hand."

"It seems you do not have very high expectations of me, madam."

He pressed his lips hard, but failed to fully contain an inelegant snort.

"Do not take that tone with me, young woman. I will not have it." Lady Matlock drove her elbows into the table and rose up on them.

Elizabeth stood and clutched the back of the chair. "Excuse me, madam, perhaps you have you forgotten, I am Mrs. Darcy. You may refer to Georgiana as 'young woman' if you wish, but I will not have you cast that appellation at me."

Lady Matlock's face flushed crimson, and she trembled. "I am not accustomed to being spoken to in such a manner."

"Neither was Lady Catherine. I assure you, it did her no lasting harm."

Lady Matlock choked on her words, sputtering, just as Lady Catherine had done, even sharing the same high coloring. How comfortingly familiar.

"I have no doubt she told you in great detail what I said to her on the day she assaulted my character at Longbourn. The same principle I addressed to her applies this day as well."

"Exactly what principle do you believe applies?"

"I am unconcerned with the opinions offered by someone so wholly unconnected with me."

"Unconnected? How dare you? We are family to Darcy! Family! How can you consider us unconnected? Have you forgotten we are peers? What better connections do you hope to have?" Lady Matlock swept her arm before her, nearly knocking over the glasses on the table.

"There are no bonds here of mutual respect or affection, only bonds of blood which are neither formed nor severed by choice. You are connected to us … to me, because you have no alternative. You have made your feelings on the matter entirely clear."

"What feelings? I have said nothing about feeling. What has sensibility to do with anything here?"

Elizabeth's knuckles turned white and her hands trembled, shaking the whole chair. "You have insulted me in every possible way. What more can you have to say to me?"

"Darcy!" Lady Matlock shrieked.

Elizabeth looked over her shoulder. Darcy stood in the doorway, jaw agape and eyes bulging.

"You will not permit your wife to speak to me thus. I will not have it, not a moment more."

Darcy looked from his aunt to Elizabeth, a deep flush creeping up his jaw. His neck corded and his jaw clenched.

Previously, she had only seen that expression when Wickham was mentioned.

"What am I seeing?" His voice was measured, deep and tense.

"What you are seeing is ... is ... is nothing at all. Absolutely nothing." Elizabeth sprinted past him, brushing his shoulder as she went.

He tried to grasp her hand, but she snatched it away and pelted for the kitchen.

She caught a scullery maid and sent her for outer-wear and her work basket. Rain or not, she could not spend another minute in this house.

At least something was going in her favor, the rain had faded to a mere drizzle. She ventured out, pulling her pelisse closed.

Darcy did not like her to walk alone. He insisted a maid or, better, a footman attend her whenever she traveled beyond the gardens.

This morning, she had to be alone.

"You would permit her to speak to me in that manner, Darcy?" Aunt Matlock turned on him with a harpy's fury.

Darcy turned to Fitzwilliam. "What happened?"

"The mistress of your household stood her ground against an invading army and the invader was taken by surprise."

"Invader!" Lady Matlock slapped the table. China clinked and rattled. "How dare you speak of your mother thus? I will not have it."

Fitzwilliam stood and tipped his head. "I shall happily accede to your wishes, madam."

He sauntered past Darcy.

Darcy trailed him into the study.

Fitzwilliam dropped into Darcy's favorite chair and crossed his legs. "Bloody hell man! Your wife is all spit and fire. Did she really say those things to Aunt Catherine?"

"Aunt Catherine went to Longbourn and confronted Elizabeth before we were betrothed."

"What I would have done to bear witness to that encounter."

"Our aunt was gravely displeased and her gracious sensibilities wounded. I bore a great deal of our aunt's ire at the incident."

"You do not seem to disapprove, though."

"Hardly. It taught me to hope as I had not before that Elizabeth might accept my second offer of marriage."

"Second offer?"

"Yes. I proposed to her once, in Kent, and she refused me."

Fitzwilliam dropped his foot hard and sat very straight. "I cannot believe it."

"She was entirely right to do so. I was insufferable."

"She refused you! Well that does put an interesting spin on it all, does it not? No one would believe any woman, particular not one in her station, would refuse a proposal from you."

"Thank you ever so much." Darcy sat on the edge of his desk. "Now tell me what did I just walk in on?"

"In short, mother insisted upon inspecting the plans for the ball and picnic. She intimated Elizabeth had no idea, whatsoever, what she was doing. Elizabeth disagreed and mother did not like it."

Darcy raked his hair out of his face. "I imagine not. Aunt Matlock is not accustomed to being challenged."

"Even father avoids disagreement with her where he can. Elizabeth charged in like a general on a black charger, sword drawn and cannons firing."

"I have been trying to keep them apart. Why do you think I insist on joining them in the drawing room every evening? I have been dreading just such an occurrence."

"The question is now, whom will you mollify first? No doubt both women will need soothing."

"Your mother is Uncle Matlock's problem, not mine." Darcy clutched his forehead.

"Do not expect much remedy there. Usually he only upsets her more, unless he buys her some sort of trinket to pacify her temper. Is there a jeweler in Lambton?"

"Not one who will suit her tastes."

"You must go to Elizabeth."

Darcy raked his hair again.

"Methinks there is a wee bit of tension there?"

Darcy flashed him a tight smile.

"Perhaps more than a wee bit."

"She has barely spoken to me since you arrived."

"I imagine that is not all she has avoided. Such a shame, too. There is a rare spark in her."

Darcy growled and slapped his desk.

"No wonder you are so tense. A married man should not—"

"Another word and I will throw your body out."

"You should try. The exercise would do you good … and thoroughly routing you would do me good."

Tempting though it was, something in Fitzwilliam's eyes suggested it would be a very bad idea to try.

Darcy broke eye contact. "Forgive me, I forget myself."

"Indeed you do. A little levity never used to distress you like this."

"We were never talking about my wife before." Darcy stared at the ceiling.

There was a fine crack in the plaster. When had that happened?

"Tell me."

"I am at wits' end. She will not see me, will not speak to me. I feel as though she is running from me at every opportunity. I have no idea why."

"No idea? Surely you cannot be so thick."

"Enlighten me. I have done everything in my power to shield her from Aunt Matlock's disapproval. I expected some appreciation for my efforts, not this."

Fitzwilliam pressed the back of his hand to his mouth, but it did nothing to quell his laughter. "Appreciated? Oh, Darce you truly have no idea, have you? Has it been so long since your mother's passing that you have no idea how a mistress runs a household?"

"What are you talking about? Mrs. Reynolds has done a completely satisfactory job running Pemberley all these years. No one has ever voiced a complaint, including myself."

"I am not talking about a housekeeper, but a mistress."

"I do not have the pleasure of understanding you."

"You employ a steward, do you not? He manages what you give him, but the estate is not his."

"You are stating the obvious."

Fitzwilliam lifted his hand. "Bear with me a moment. The steward may take pride in his management, but it is not an extension of himself, not the way Pemberley is to you. If another, say my father, were to criticize how you managed the fields or the fences, would you take umbrage?"

"Of course, how dare he suppose to know what is best for my estate."

"Exactly. That is what you have done."

"Ridiculous."

"How many times have you stepped into Elizabeth's offices to directly manage affairs as you would have them to be?"

"I am master of the house. Is it not my—"

"Yes, it is your right to have things as you wish them to be. Yet, it is a matter of respect to not usurp her authority. My mother would never tolerate Father directly informing the housekeeper of what to serve. At dinner, when you declare we shall all withdraw together? Oh, Darcy." Fitzwilliam leaned back and shook his head.

"I am only protecting Elizabeth."

"You are declaring her an insufficient hostess in front of her guests. Allow her to handle matters. If you desire to say such a thing, it should be communicated in private."

"That is absurd."

"What other man have you ever seen do as you have done."

"I never paid attention."

"Of course you did not. You should not have had to; it is obvious."

No it was not. Few things were. Darcy dragged his hand over his face.

"You know I do not grasp such things easily. Mother … she always explained the workings of these matters. I expected she had taught me all I needed to know."

"Apparently she did not. I only hope it is not too late for you to learn."

The rain remained at a steady drizzle, enough to be noticeable and annoying, painting her eyelashes and cheeks, but not enough to actively take shelter against it. Even if it increased, she would not bother to hide from it. The clouds so effectively expressed the content of her soul, how could she deny their opportunity for expression?

She brushed raindrops from her eyes. What could excuse the conversation she just had with Lady Matlock? Madness perhaps, but short of that, nothing.

No doubt, the lady herself would prefer never to see her again. Small loss that would be. But surely her display must have cost Darcy's good opinion of her.

That loss …

She increased her pace, going nowhere in particular. At least she would get there quickly.

Still, she had to go back to Pemberley at some time. Then what? How would she explain her unseemly display? How would she apologize?

A large puddle opened before her. She dodged it. Her feet slipped from under her and she fell backwards. The ground sloped and she tumbled down a squat embankment and landed in a small stream.

Her head spun, and pain assaulted her from multiple angles. Cold penetrated her limbs.

Water.

She was in the water. That could kill her sooner than anything else. On elbows and knees, she crawled out of the frigid stream.

A low branch hung over her head. She grabbed it and tried to drag herself to her feet, but a searing pain in her ankle drove her to her knees.

She cried out, but no one could hear. No one knew her whereabouts or even that she had gone.

A sharp breeze cut through the trees, chilling the sopping fabric clinging to her legs. The temperatures would drop quickly once the sun went down, not long from now. Somehow, she had to get back to Pemberley before dark.

Darcy paced across the front of the study's fireplace, dodging Fitzwilliam, the one thing in the room not in its proper place, as he went.

"Sir, I do not know where she has gone." Mrs. Reynolds wrung her hands. "She left with her work basket, through the kitchen, but made no mention of where she would be calling."

Mrs. Reynolds had never looked so small or so old.

Georgiana pushed her way into the study. "Is it true, brother? Elizabeth is missing?"

"We do not know," Fitzwilliam said.

Darcy took a deep breath. "She left without a servant to accompany her, and none knows where she went."

"But how could she do that? You are so adamant that neither of us is to go out alone. Are you very angry with her?"

"This is not helpful, Georgiana." Fitzwilliam's tone dropped to something low and severe.

"You do not need to be harsh with me. It is not as though I have done something very bad. Surely she will be back soon, will she not? Are you not worrying for nothing?"

Sometimes it was clear, Georgiana was still a child.

"I will look for her." Darcy strode toward the door.

"No you will not. That is utter foolishness." Aunt Matlock shouldered her way inside. "The girl stormed off in a huff over the preparations for a ball. Leave her to her own devices. If something happens to her, then it is entirely her own fault. She will learn better sense."

"Mother! How can you say—"

"It is complete nonsense the way she is carrying on. I do not see how you permit it, Darcy. Truly I do not." Aunt waved her hand as though to dismiss him.

Darcy towered over her. "I did not invite you into my study. I would thank you to get out. Now."

"You will not speak to me that way, nephew."

"This is my house, and I will speak to you as I wish. You may choose to be a respectful guest in my home, or you may choose to keep to your rooms, or you may choose to leave. At this moment, I care not which. I am going to look for my wife." He pushed his way through the doorway, calling for his great coat and horse.

A chill, sharp wind whipped up dirt and leaves on the path from the house. He met the grooms halfway to the stable and mounted.

What direction would she have gone? There was no telling. One was as good as the next.

A west wind pelted his face with stinging drizzle. Someone had said something about sickness in the western cottages. Perhaps she called there. He turned his horse into the wind and trotted off.

Few were on the roads, but every soul he encountered, he asked the same thing. None had seen her. The cottagers and the two farmers on the west-most farms promised to keep watch for her but had no other news to soothe his angst.

The people of Pemberley already seemed to know her. And they loved her, as they had loved his mother. How many remarked she knew them by name and remembered their needs.

Darcy swallowed hard. After they began calling on the tenants, she wrote notes on their visits and studied them every night. It was no accident that she was familiar with those who lived on Pemberley, but the product of intentional and effortful study.

What more could he ask from the mistress of his estate? She had discerned what was most important to him and made that dear to herself as well. A partner in the fullest sense of the word.

What would he do without her?

His hands went numb and his head swam.

No, no! That thought was not at all helpful. It would paralyze him, and for Elizabeth's sake, that would not do.

He turned his horse toward the manor, cold, wet and alone.

Entirely and completely alone. More alone than he had ever been before he met Elizabeth.

Fitzwilliam's words rubbed raw places in his soul as he rode. Fitzwilliam was right. He had run rough-shod over Elizabeth's authority and place in his home.

What must she believe of him? That he was a boorish brute?

That was not wholly untrue.

Worse, she must be certain he had no faith in in her, that everything he told her was a lie.

How he hated deception. Could she believe it of him?

Given the circumstances, she certainly had reason to. That could not continue.

Pray let her be safe and warm at the house when he arrived.

Mrs. Reynolds met him at the door with the news he least wanted. Elizabeth had not returned. Sundown was approaching and with it, the likelihood of tragedy.

He called for Fitzwilliam. "Gather all the men. We must form a party to search for her."

Fitzwilliam's bearing changed. Gone was his reck-less cousin and in his place stood one of His Majesty's finest.

He stroked his chin. "She was on foot; she could not have gone very far. She is probably escaping from the weather in a cottager's house, or at one of the farms. You only searched to the west, did you not? There are many other places she could take refuge." He grasped Darcy's wrist. "She is well, I am sure."

Sampson burst into the study. "Sir, a group of carolers approaches."

"Carolers?" Darcy cursed under his breath. "Send them away. I do not need the distraction.

Sampson turned on his heel.

Fitzwilliam reached for the butler's shoulder. "Wait, wait, no, bring them in. Perhaps one of them knows where—"

"Yes, that is an excellent idea," Darcy said.

"Mr. Darcy!"

That was Mrs. Reynolds' shriek from the vestibule. She never raised her voice!

He pelted from his study, Fitzwilliam on his heels.

A group of men and a few women, ten perhaps, shuffled in the front hall.

"Here, sir!" Mrs. Reynolds waved at him.

Steadman and his eldest son carried Elizabeth between them.

"We found her, sir, on the way caroling, fallen near the stream, barely conscious." Mrs. Steadman plucked at the edges of her shawl.

He took Elizabeth from them, her skin cold and clammy to the touch. Her gown clung wetly to her legs, soaked through with mud. She moaned in his arms.

She lived!

"Upstairs! Blankets and hot water, immediately!" He clutched her to him, willing his warmth to cut through her chill.

"I will see the carolers to the kitchen, sir. Mrs. Darcy set aside provisions in case they came." Mrs.

Reynolds marshalled her forces into action, and maids scurried about.

Darcy trundled toward the stairs.

"You must get her warm and dry, quickly. She has been out in the cold far too long." Fitzwilliam ran beside him and opened their chamber door.

Her maid stood ready, towels in hand. She tried to shoo him way as she undressed Elizabeth, but he remained rooted in place, helping as he could. He had been turned away too many times recently. This time, he would not capitulate.

Elizabeth began to shiver, her teeth chattering so hard she could not speak. He wrapped her in another blanket and then in his arms and they sat on the rug before the fire.

The maid pressed a cup of hot tea into her shaking hands. Darcy steadied them and held the cup to her lips.

"Drink it, it will help warm you."

Surely she did not need to be told such a thing. But he had to say something.

At last the shivering stopped, and she breathed normally again. He tucked her head under his chin and held her.

Mrs. Reynolds peeked in. "The carolers, sir. They are asking after the mistress. Would you be willing to—"

"There is no need."

Elizabeth stirred. "Yes, pray go to them. They … they need to … to know what they did … that it means something."

She pulled away from him, as though trying to stand.

"You cannot go. You cannot even stand now. The surgeon must be called for your ankle."

"They cannot think you do not appreciate …"

The blanket fell from her shoulders.

Mrs. Reynolds rushed to replace it. "Pray, sir. It would ease the mistress's mind."

"Allow me to help you to bed, and then I will go."

"Thank you."

He carried her to their bed and gently set her down. His arms ached with the loss of her warmth. It had been far too long since he had held her.

They could not go back to their previous separation.

He pressed a kiss to her forehead. "We must talk when I return."

"I will stay with her, sir." Mrs. Reynolds tucked the counterpane over her shoulders.

He dragged himself to the doorway. She would not speak with him if he did not see to the carolers first, and they must speak.

They waited for him at the base of the grand stair. He stopped several steps above them. So many worried faces looked up at him.

"The mistress is improving. The surgeon will be called for, but we expect her to fully recover. I cannot express our gratitude for your help."

Smiles and polite cheers broke out among the group. Mr. Steadman, at the front center of the group, turned to the rest and nodded. They stilled a moment and then sang.

Joy to the World was a fitting hymn and *We Wish you a Merry Christmas* was an excellent sentiment.

Bless Sampson for escorting them out before they could begin another.

That done, he would send for the surgeon, and he and Elizabeth would talk. Then all would return to as it should be.

Darcy straightened his coat and strode back to his chamber.

Mrs. Reynolds met him at the door way. "She is sleeping, sir. I think it best not to wake her."

"See the surgeon is here first thing in the morning. You may inform our guests, should they ask, I am retiring for the evening."

"Yes, sir." She curtsied and left.

He closed the door and entered through the dressing room. His valet met him there and assisted his nightly ablutions. Was the man particularly slow this night, or did they always take so long?

The door between the dressing room and his chamber whispered creaks as he opened it. Even the door knew not to disturb her.

He stepped in, stopping just three steps inside. Her soft breaths filled the room. In the dim glow of the moonlight, he could just make out her form under heaps of blankets.

He held back the cry lodged in his throat. Thank Providence she was there.

Careful not to disturb her warmth, he slipped in beside her. Should he move closer, or would that wake her? Would she pull away from him once again?

He slid nearer drawn, a moth to a flame. How could she be so close and not in his arms?

She murmured and stirred.

He held his breath and lay perfectly still. Pray, let her not pull away.

She inched a little closer. He tucked his arm under her head. She nestled into his shoulder and sighed a contented little sound like she used to every night.

Now things were right once again.

❧ Chapter 5

HIS VALET STOOD BESIDE the bed and cleared his throat.

Darcy groaned and rubbed his eyes, a bright sunbeam directly on his face. When had it become daylight?

"Sir, the surgeon is come."

"Help me dress." Darcy rolled from under the covers, watchful to tuck them back around her.

"What ..." She rolled toward him, groaning.

"The surgeon will see you shortly. Do not get up." He patted her shoulder, or at least what he thought might be her shoulder under the heavy counterpane.

A quarter hour later, Mrs. Reynolds showed the surgeon in.

Darcy briefly described what had happened and what had been done.

"I am here, you know. It is possible for me to answer questions as well." Elizabeth pulled herself up on a pile of pillows and peeked at them.

How worn her expression. Her skin was dull, even a bit ashen, matching her voice.

Heavens, let there be nothing seriously wrong.

The surgeon shuffled to her side and began his examination. He walked like a crow, picking up his feet a might too high and stretching out each step in a very purposeful way. His elbows, knees and chin were sharp and pointed as a lancet's blade. She shivered as he removed the blankets and cried out when he touched her ankle.

"Is it broken?" she whispered, clutching the sheets to her.

He poked and prodded and stared and muttered. "I do not believe so. You are quite fortunate. It would not have been surprising if it had been. Still, I fear the cold may have settled on you. We must watch careful for any sign of a fever or cough."

"I … I feel fine, save for the ankle."

"You may believe you do, madam, but it would not be wise to take any chances with your health. I recommend you keep to your bed and not walk at all for at least a week. I will instruct your maid as to the poultices and wraps she must use on your ankle."

"Might I use walking sticks? I cannot imagine—"

"Not for at least a se'nnight complete, madam, perhaps more. We must ascertain the extent of the injury. Then, we can determine what means are safe for you."

She fell back into the pillows, groaning.

"Pray, do not disobey my orders. It is far too easy to exacerbate the injury and cause more damage in the process. If you do, it could be months before you are able to walk comfortably, even years."

"Months?" She gasped.

"I have seen cases that never healed properly. If you do not wish to be one of those cases, follow my orders precisely. I will also leave you a preparation of laudanum for the pain which will increase over the course of the next day or so."

She closed her eyes and nodded.

The surgeon beckoned Darcy to the dressing room and shut the door between the rooms.

"She is fortunate to have been found when she was. The cold and damp might have killed her otherwise. She will be weak for some time. Keep her warm and calm at all costs. Upsetting her could result in a dangerous brain fever."

"I understand."

"Make sure your staff understands as well. And your guests. I have seen situations where guests cause sufficient agitation to impair a lady's health. To be sure, I know nothing of your situation. I am not speaking in particulars, only in generalities."

Of course he was.

"I will instruct my staff" … and his relatives … "accordingly."

"Very good sir. I will provide your housekeeper and Mrs. Darcy's maid with instructions and a tincture for Mrs. Darcy. Unless you call for me, I shall return in two days' time to check her progress."

Darcy called for Mrs. Reynolds. She saw the surgeon out, and he returned to Elizabeth.

She sat up in bed, a pretty shawl over her shoulders. But her face was pale and lines creased beside her eyes.

"The surgeon will call the day after tomorrow."

"I understand." Her voice was a whisper, a shadow of its usual brightness.

He perched on the bed beside her and searched for her hand under the blankets. "He said you must be kept warm and—"

"And not agitated. I heard."

"I shall speak—"

"There is no need, I am well."

"I hardly think that the case." He squeezed her hand, so cold and small in his. "Why did you run off yesterday?"

She closed her eyes and turned aside. "I was foolish."

"Elizabeth, I have never considered you a fool. What happened?"

"Nothing you need to concern yourself about. It was entirely my fault. I will keep myself under better regulation in the future."

"My aunt is a difficult person."

Ah, that earned a direct gaze.

His heart beat a little faster.

"I have always considered her difficult to tolerate. My mother was also apt to clash with her. She never saw eye to eye with either Lady Catherine or with Aunt Matlock. Surely she wrote of it somewhere her journals. You must have read that."

"No, I have seen nothing of the sort among them."

"I am surprised, given the heat of the discussions I witnessed when they thought I was not looking."

"I think she preferred to write of pleasing things."

Darcy laced his fingers in hers. If there were any measure of truth in Fitzwilliam's warnings, he had best approach this lightly.

"The surgeon said you should not exert yourself and you should not be taxed."

"I heard." She shifted on the bed only to wince and reach for her ankle.

"I see wisdom in his suggestion." He kept his voice very soft. "A ball this year may not be possible."

She squeezed her eyes shut and pressed the back of her hand to her lips.

"It would be very disappointing if the hostess could not dance at her own ball. Now I am married, I will dance with none but you. I should like to inform Mrs. Reynolds we are going to cancel the event. If you agree, of course."

"You are correct. It would be good of you to inform her. Notice should be sent out immediately." She sucked in several deep breaths.

He brushed stray hairs from her forehead. "I know this is not what you would have preferred, though I think it for the best. I shall inform her now."

It was disappointing to be sure, but what choice did they have? At least she seemed resigned to it and did not resent his interference. That was something.

Perhaps now, Aunt's meddling would cease and peace might return to Pemberley.

Elizabeth listened for the door to close. She peeked through half closed eyes.

He was gone.

She curled into a tight ball despite the searing pain in her ankle. How could she have done such a thing? To have to be rescued by a passing band of carolers! Even if they were tenants of the estate, it was little better than the plot of some ridiculous gothic novel.

The valiant heroine flees from the evil castle, only to become horribly injured in her flight. Not to fear, the valiant hero is come to her rescue and put everything to right once again.

Carolers were not valiant heroes, just good Samaritans of the Christmastide season. Nothing was made right by her return to Pemberley.

Perhaps it was for the best they canceled the ball.

Certainly that would satisfy Aunt Matlock's concerns. It sounded like it would be a relief to Darcy as well.

But the humiliation of recanting invitations after they had been sent! No doubt word of her foolish accident would be circulating the estate now. All would know it was her fault their season's merriment was lost.

What an auspicious beginning. One that would be talked about for years to come.

Aunt Matlock would never let her forget. And Lady Catherine! Elizabeth shuddered. The next time she was at Rosings, the topic would be rehashed until she fled screaming from the room.

If she could manage to walk again.

She eased her leg out from under the covers and examined her ankle.

Swollen and multicolored, quite a sight to behold. She ran her fingers along the swelling.

Heavens above that hurt!

She wiggled her toes.

No, no! That was no better. Pressing her foot lightly to the mattress was definitely much worse.

The surgeon was right. She could not walk on it, not for some time.

Botheration!

Now denied her one escape, she was trapped with the Matlocks, and with Darcy.

What was she to do with him? How could she possibly share his room? Bad enough merely knowing how disappointed he was, but to face him so closely?

There must be some way to return to the mistress's chamber.

Fitzwilliam strode into the study without knocking. "I saw the surgeon take leave."

"He pronounced her ankle sprained, but sound." Darcy rose from behind his desk.

"That is a great relief. Too many surgeons are too handy with their bone saws. I have no wish to see—or hear—such ever again." Fitzwilliam dropped into the chair nearest the fire, color drained from his face.

Darcy poured him a half glass of brandy.

Fitzwilliam drank it in a single gulp. He covered his eyes with his hand.

"Are you well?"

His voice dropped very low. "Some things pull me back to France, whether I wish to go or not."

Darcy pulled a chair a little closer and sat beside him. "Forgive me for bringing the reminder."

"It is hardly your fault. I can think of few places less like France than Pemberley. Surgeons though, I dread them like the very devil himself." He kneaded his left shoulder.

Darcy's brows rose high. "I had no idea you were wounded. Why did you never tell me?"

"Not the kind of thing to share, especially when my mother might discover it. Fought the damn surgeon for days to keep my arm. I think of it enough on my own. I need not have her constant reminders plaguing me."

Darcy refilled Fitzwilliam's glass and poured a second for himself.

"Are you fully recovered?"

"As much as I will ever be. Just do not ask me to go hunting with you anymore." Fitzwilliam hunched over his lap and rolled the glass back and forth between his palms.

"The shoulder?"

"And the gunfire. Cannot abide it." He shuddered. "What of Elizabeth?"

"The surgeon declared she should not be taxed during her recovery. She is to stay off her feet entirely for a week at least."

"How convenient for her to avoid my parents. I shall recommend it to other relatives when visits are arranged." He cocked his head, his crooked grin returned.

Maddening, but a distinct improvement,

"You do not think Cousin Anne would happily throw herself down to the stairs to avoid seeing my mother?"

"She is already an invalid and needs no additional excuse." Darcy sipped his drink.

It was very early for brandy.

"I suggested to Elizabeth we cancel the ball."

"Call off the ball? Surely not."

"I can hardly see another way. If she is not to be burdened and must keep to bed, how might she possibly be able to manage it—"

"Without giving it over to my mother's control."

"My thoughts precisely."

"If Mother took the reins, Elizabeth would forever be fighting for her rights as Mistress of Pemberley. Of course, you are right. Dare I ask what she said?"

"She agreed with me."

Fitzwilliam cocked his head and stared at him with a wrinkled half frown. "She simply agreed with you? No discussion? That hardly sounds like the woman who confronted my mother yesterday."

"She seemed unhappy about it, but she did not argue."

"And you asked her, not told her?"

"I did listen to you yesterday. Yes, I asked."

Fitzwilliam sipped his brandy. "I am astonished you would be so easily swayed to change. Good on you."

"I like to think I am not entirely unredeemable."

"I as well. I have given up hope for my parents and my brother the Viscount."

"You are ever so much the font of cheer and sunshine."

"Pleased to render whatever service I am able." Fitzwilliam lifted his glass. "Would you like assistance in breaking the news to my mother?"

"That is a very good idea. Shall we?"

Fitzwilliam downed the last of his drink and led the way to the morning room.

Aunt Matlock sat near the window, reading the society pages. She peered over the paper at them.

"I heard of all the foolishness last night. It is a very great wonder Mrs. Darcy did not kill herself with her impetuous actions."

"Thank you for your concern, it is good of you to ask after her welfare." Fitzwilliam sat opposite her, settling in, hands clasped, as though preparing for the opening act at the theater.

"I do not appreciate your sarcasm, son."

Fitzwilliam rolled his eyes.

"I hope you have had a stern talk with your wife, Darcy. She must be kept in check. I cannot imagine where she acquired her manners from, but it is simply not to be borne. She may be Mrs. Darcy, but that does not excuse the rudeness … the impertinence she exhibited yesterday. One might even surmise the accident that befell her is Providence's little reminder she should better understand who her betters are and be more cautious in her treatment of them."

Darcy clenched his fists until his hands ached. "I will not discuss this and would thank you to keep such opinions to yourself."

"Your mother would be ashamed of you Darcy and your father, too. I cannot understand what has become of you. It must be the low influence of your new connections. I insist—"

"You are in no place to insist upon anything. I require that you stop at once. I should remind you, you are a guest in my home and that deserves your respect."

Aunt Matlock sputtered and flapped like a wet hen. All she needed was a feathered turban to complete the impression.

"I came only to apprise you of the change in our plans as per the surgeon's orders. My wife will be abed at least a week and will be unable to manage the plans for the ball."

"So you wish me to take over? High time you recognized the need for a more experienced hand—"

"Nothing of the sort. We are calling off the ball altogether."

Aunt Matlock rose to her full, though rather inconsiderable, height. Was she trying to be intimidating?

"That is without a doubt the most ridiculous thing I have ever heard. There is no need to cancel. What will the county, nay the *ton* think? You will be the laughing stock—"

"You are not going to carry off the ball in her stead."

"Of course I am. Georgiana is not up to the task. I have barely had sight of the girl since we have been here. Send Mrs. Reynolds to me—"

"There will be no ball this year and that is the final word on the matter." Darcy turned his back and marched out.

She followed him from morning room to parlor, and from parlor to study, arguing for her way. Up the stairs, to the gallery, through the music room and the library, she insisted the ball was a privilege, no, her very right to arrange. It would be the height of cruelty to take it from her. She invoked the names of his parents, and even tried to insist that the Almighty himself required Darcy to yield.

He would not be moved.

Neither, though, would she.

They faced each other, at an impasse, in front of Uncle Matlock's chamber.

Darcy pounded the door with his fist. "Your presence is required immediately, sir."

Grumbling and shuffling echoed from within and the door flew open.

"What the devil do you want, Darcy? No need to bellow at a man in his own room." Uncle Matlock tied the belt of his banyan firmly around his waist. He leaned against the doorframe, lifting his gouty foot slightly.

"Your wife, sir." Darcy gestured with both hands toward Aunt Matlock.

"I am well aware of who she is."

"I require you to manage her."

Aunt Matlock moved to wedge herself between them, but Darcy shouldered her aside.

"Managed? I, Managed? How dare you suggest—"

Uncle Matlock's head lolled to the side and his lips wrinkled into a crooked line. "I have been attempting that unsuccessfully for years. How exactly do you propose I succeed at it now?"

"Frankly I do not care—"

She pressed between them. "I am standing right here, I will not have you speak of me as though I were not."

"That, sir is your trouble and not mine. Inform her to accept the fact there will be no Pemberley ball this year."

"Tell your foolish nephew what a ridiculous notion that is."

"It is his house to do with as he wishes." Uncle Matlock clutched his forehead and shook his head. "Cease and desist, madam, and leave the poor man to his own." He turned and shuffled back into the darkened room.

"How can you say such nonsense?" Aunt followed him inside.

Darcy shut the door on them both. The heavy oak did little to dampen her strident voice on the other side.

How long had they lived like dog and cat? His shoulders twitched. Pray, however did Uncle tolerate the discord?

He did not.

Uncle Matlock spent as much time out of her company as he could. Just as many men of his station did. Most of the men of his acquaintance did the same

Pray, let he and Elizabeth never get to that same place.

He hurried down the long corridor to the family wing. With any luck, she would not be sleeping. Even if she was, he would sit with her. Just her presence would soothe the rawness left in his aunt's wake.

Several maids fussed in the dressing room, moving in and out from the mistress's chambers.

"What are you doing?" he asked.

"The mistress requested her room be freshened for her."

Her room?

He dodged the busy staff and ducked into his chambers. Elizabeth sat propped on pillows, a book in her lap. Her eyes, though, were fixed on something beyond the window.

She did not turn toward him.

"Elizabeth? What are the maids doing?" He sat beside her and took her hand in his.

Her hands were so very cold. She tried to slip them away, but he held her firmly.

She opened her mouth as though to speak, but closed it again and shrugged.

"Are you uncomfortable here? I thought you found this chamber more appealing. But if you desire, we may move to the other."

She looked over his shoulder into the dressing room.

"You do not wish to be with me?" The words tore from him like flesh rending from his chest.

She sniffled and shook her head. What did she mean?

"It is not fair for your sleep to be disturbed. The laudanum leaves me restive and fitful during the night."

"Is that not something best left for me to decide? It is my sleep after all."

"I hate the thought of being a … a burden to you."

He leaned closer into her face, but she refused to meet his gaze. "I hate the thought of being apart."

"But does it not make more sense? You will worry every time you roll over that you are hurting me. How can you possibly rest that way?"

Dash it all, why would she not look at him?

He rose and closed the door to the dressing room. Back against the door, he crossed his arms and studied her.

She huddled deep into the pillows, arms drawn tight to her chest.

"I have not had a decent night's sleep since you moved to the mistress' chambers."

"You have not?" She peered at him, eyes wide.

He strode toward her. "No. I quite dislike it."

"I had no idea."

"Now you know. Do you still wish to remove to the mistress' chambers?" He leaned on the bed, close to her face, voice very soft. "I shall not stop you if you truly wish it. But I demand you look at me, directly in the eye. Tell me that is what you truly desire"

Slowly, agonizingly slowly, she met his gaze, as shyly as if she had never looked into his eyes before.

"I … that is to say … I would prefer …" She licked her lips. "No, that is not what I most desire."

He released the aching breath trapped in his chest. "Then it is settled. I shall inform the maid the room is not immediately needed. Is there something from there which may be brought here for your comfort?"

"Pray do not trouble yourself."

"Perhaps the fainting couch? It will fit along the window. It might help you to sit there and you could look out upon the grounds. You would have light enough to read and sew whilst you keep off your feet."

"That would be far too much trouble and would require too much disarray of your rooms. I know how much you dislike—"

"Pray, let me do this for you. Nothing would give me greater pleasure than to be able to increase your comfort. I know how much you dislike confinement. Do not deny me this." He clasped her hands and brought them close to his heart.

"I would appreciate it very much."

He pressed his forehead to hers. "I shall make arrangements immediately. Thank you."

Aunt Matlock kept to her chambers for the next several few days.

Was it wrong that these were by far the most pleasant evenings Darcy had spent since the Matlocks arrived? Enjoying port, cigars, and talk of race horses and sport over dinner without fear of offending the ladies held particular appeal. Especially after all the stilted conversation Aunt Matlock had presided over.

If only Elizabeth were able to join them, or even Georgiana, but one was unable and the other unwilling. Perhaps if Aunt Matlock continued to stay away, he could persuade Georgiana to come join them.

Three days later, Mrs. Reynolds and a maid carrying a supper tray came to their bedchamber. Mrs. Reynolds pulled a table near the fainting couch and directed the girl to place the tray and leave.

"I was skeptical about fitting another piece of furniture into this room, but it seems to have worked out in the end. The Master has a way about him, figuring out such things. Perhaps, even after you have recovered, you may decide to keep things this way. It does add a nice feminine touch to this room. Are you comfortable, Madam?"

Poor woman, she must be quite concerned. She rarely said so much in a single breath.

"Yes, it is very comfortable. I had not realized how much it would help to be near the window." Elizabeth pushed herself up a little straighter.

The view from the windows was much more appealing than staring at the paneled walls of the Master's chambers.

"The Master is thoughtful, is he not? And such a gracious host now the men have been dining together these last few nights."

"Lady Matlock is still not among them?"

"No, she has kept to her rooms recently. As I understand, she suffers with a headache this evening. It is entirely possible that her headache could last a week complete. They have been known to in the past."

"How interesting. Are you aware, perhaps, of what brings on these headaches?"

Even Mama would have been impressed at the sweetness of her tone.

"They are often preceded by failure to find satisfaction in a turn of events."

Perhaps this was the model for Georgiana's behavior.

"She and Mr. Darcy still do not see eye to eye regarding the ball?"

"Not as I am given to understand. It is true, there will be some general disappointment all around, but none will hold it against you. We have received a number of notes already inquiring after your health. Ever so many have worried about you once news of your accident circulated."

She blushed hot, her cheeks prickling.

"These things happen, that is the way of the world." Mrs. Reynolds poured a cup of tea and handed it to her. "The Lady Anne once fell from her horse in front of the church when a dog spooked the beast. She injured her shoulder in the fall and was unable to pay calls for near a month complete. There was widespread consternation over her health after that."

One more thing Lady Anne never committed to her journals.

"Has Georgiana stirred from her rooms?"

"No, madam. She remains locked away. Mrs. Annesley says that she is quite content to be so."

"Does Mrs. Annesley at least continue her lessons during her isolation?"

"I believe she tries, but—"

"Miss Darcy feels too frail to undertake such efforts. She fears a brain fever might ensue, I suppose?" Elizabeth sipped her tea, eyes closed, lest she been seen rolling them.

"Mrs. Annesley thinks it unlikely and is loath to permit the excuse, but …"

"Mr. Darcy accepts it."

"That is Miss Darcy's explanation, madam. But, do not trouble yourself with that now. The surgeon is expected soon. You might wish to have your supper first."

The possibility of good news whetted her appetite, and Elizabeth ate, watching the window for the surgeon's gig.

The surgeon pronounced it safe enough to attempt to walk using walking sticks. Darcy brought them to her and hung about like a mother hen as she hobbled across the room.

While she could manage to traverse a short distance, she would not be going far. The stairs were certainly out of the question, but the entire first floor of the house was now open to her.

After the surgeon's visit, Darcy suggested a stroll through the gallery. By stroll, he meant a slow, tottering shamble, but still, it was better than sitting. The change of scenery alone improved her mood dramatically.

Since her accident, he had been so patient, so solicitous, with little trace of dissatisfaction with her. It was like having the man she knew as her husband back again.

"I know the stares of my ancestors are nothing to the outdoors, but at least the coolness of this chamber reminds one of fresh air." He hovered very close to her side.

Though the attentions were mildly suffocating, the walking sticks were difficult to manage and the security of his strong arms nearby proved welcome.

"Indeed it does. I have been far too long in a single room and fear that Bedlam beckons. Tell me of our guests."

"Fitzwilliam is quite sanguine in all things. He is not difficult to please. A bit of peace in the countryside with nothing to remind him of France, and he is a happy man."

"I understand your aunt still complains of a headache and keeps much to her rooms."

"She does, but I am not sure anyone truly minds. The surgeon called upon her as well today. I believe she availed herself of one of his laudanum potions."

Elizabeth shook her head hard enough to threaten her balance. "While they are indeed effective at relieving pain, I find they bring more discomfort than relief. Every time I drink it, oh, how I itch, and my mouth feels stuffed with cotton wool." She smacked her lips and worked her tongue over the roof of her mouth.

"It seemed you must have had strange dreams, too, disturbing ones at that. You were very restless those nights."

"I feared I might have disturbed your sleep. Are you certain—"

He caught her upper arm in his strong hand, gentle and warm, but sure and unwavering.

"Absolutely. Even when you are restless, I sleep far better with you beside me."

She paused to catch her breath, arms aching from the walking sticks.

"Uncle certainly seems more agreeable for Aunt's use of the draughts. He barely complained about his gout or anything else over breakfast. What is more, Mrs. Annesley brought Georgiana down to the breakfast table this morning. She has not appeared for any other meals, but this is a start. I am hopeful it will continue."

Hopeful? It was by his approval that she kept to herself.

"The Gardiners are supposed to arrive tomorrow. The nursery is in order for the children and their nursery maid. But as to your aunt and uncle, what might be done for their comfort?"

Oh, that.

She sagged against the walking sticks.

"What rooms have you instructed Mrs. Reynolds to prepare for them?"

He stopped mid-step and stared at her. "What do you mean?"

"My aunt and uncle will require chambers."

"Have you not made arrangements for them?"

She hobbled her way toward the window. The air was cooler there, easing the burn in her cheeks.

"Elizabeth?"

"The Earl and Lady Matlock are using those rooms," she whispered.

He walked again, hands clasped tightly behind his back, the way he paced when he was trying to puzzle something out.

"Mrs. Reynolds did not mention to you those were the rooms favored by my relations? But why would she? They were not expected. How would you have known? It should not have mattered in the first place," he muttered, barely audible.

He rarely muttered.

"Bloody hell!" He slapped his fist into his palm.

And he never cursed in her presence.

"Pray, will you tell Mrs. Reynolds where they should stay?"

He stared at her in such an odd way. What had she said so very wrong?

"Excuse me." He bowed as he did to company and strode out.

She lowered herself onto the bench below the window.

What had she done this time? She squeezed her eyes shut and pressed the back of her hands to her eyes. Hot trails traced down her cheeks.

Darcy pelted down the stairs, restraining his urge to shout for Mrs. Reynolds. She must have heard his frantic footstep, appearing at the base of the stairs as he reached them.

"Has the mistress taken ill? Has she injured herself?"

"No, no, Mrs. Darcy is quite well. We were walking in the gallery. The Gardiners, they are arriving tomorrow."

Furrows deepened beside her eyes and she took on that look, the one she had worn when he was young, and not behaving as he should.

"Yes sir."

"Their rooms?"

"The staff is prepared to make rooms ready as soon as we are directed which rooms to use."

"You had instructions previously?"

"Yes, sir."

"And I overrode those?"

"Yes sir."

"Why did you not inform me?"

"I did, sir."

He dragged his hand down his face. "In the future, Mrs. Reynolds, should I issue an order that in any way affects something Mrs. Darcy has already told you, you are to inform me directly of the conflict and direct me to speak with her on the matter before you make a change."

"Understood sir." The creases around her eyes eased a mite.

"As to accommodations for the Gardiners." He pulled at his face again. "What do you believe Mrs. Darcy would find most pleasing?"

"Have you asked her?"

"She asked—informed me—that I should make those arrangements. To that end, I require your recommendation. What would please her the most?"

"If I might be so bold as to suggest, sir. There are unused rooms in the family wing. They are not as grand as the gold suite to be sure, but those might make it easier for her to spend time with her aunt."

"Brilliant! Make it so."

She curtsied and hurried off.

Darcy leaned against the banister.

Hopefully, Elizabeth would approve and some of her melancholy would abate. Perhaps then she would talk with him again.

He wandered back to his study.

How striking that his house should be so full of people and yet he felt so very alone.

Chapter 6

LATE THE FOLLOWING MORNING, Sampson announced a carriage and luggage cart had been seen on the lane. The Gardiners, no doubt. A final check with Mrs. Reynolds ensured the rooms ready for their arrival and refreshments prepared.

How could half an hour last so very long?

He paced the parlor, dodging comfortable chairs and small tables, waiting. Why was there not a clear open path for walking the length of the room?

In his younger days, he would have been outside, running the front lawns in anticipation of company. But that was no longer considered proper.

"The Gardiners, sir." Sampson ushered them into the parlor.

Weary and dusty, the children tumbled in ahead of their parents. The four youngsters assembled themselves before him and curtsied and bowed as best as their stiff little bodies allowed.

"Mr. Gardiner, Mrs. Gardiner, I am very pleased you are come." He bowed. "I trust your journey has been a comfortable one."

"As comfortable as any long journey may be."

"Refreshments for the children are laid out in the kitchen. If you would like your nursery maid to escort them?" He smiled and glanced at his newly acquired nieces and nephews.

"Once they have eaten, if you think it fitting, they may have a ramble about the grounds. One of the young grooms can bring out the spaniels. They might have a bit of a romp with the puppies, if that would be agreeable."

"Oh yes, Papa, please!" The smallest boy ran up to his father, a hopeful look on his face.

Mr. Gardiner ruffled his hair. "I think that would be just the thing for you, son. We are most obliged, sir."

"When they are finished, the nursery has been made ready for them."

"Most kind of you, sir," Mrs. Gardiner said.

Mrs. Reynolds arrived with the nursery maid in her wake. The children followed them out.

A maid slipped in, bearing a tray of tea and refreshments. They sat down.

"Might I inquire, sir, where is Lizzy? I am a bit surprised not to see her here with us." Mrs. Gardiner asked.

"I am afraid she met with a bit of an accident."

"What happened? It is serious?"

"She slipped on some wet ground and injured her ankle. The surgeon has pronounced her well, save for that. Yesterday she was able to have a bit of an amble about the first floor, but she cannot yet manage the stairs."

Mrs. Gardiner pressed her hand to her chest and leaned back. "I am quite relieved to hear it is nothing serious. What a shame for her to be unable to enjoy her company."

"There is a sitting room that she favors upstairs. I have taken the liberty of preparing rooms for you near-by. Perhaps you may keep company with Elizabeth there."

"Most considerate of you, sir." Mr. Gardiner glanced at his wife.

She wore a quiet, thoughtful expression, very similar to Elizabeth's. What was she thinking?

"At dinner tonight, I shall introduce you to my relations, Earl and Lady Matlock."

"Indeed? We had no idea you would be hosting so large a house party, sir." Mrs. Gardiner's brows rose high. "We would certainly not have imposed our company upon you this season had we known."

"Their arrival was most unexpected."

"What an honor for Elizabeth to receive. Dinner is then a quite formal event, I imagine?" she asked.

That was one way to describe it.

"My aunt prefers it so."

"We will dress accordingly."

Darcy's jaw dropped. "Forgive me, madam. I meant not to imply … that is I meant no offense … I had not thought …"

"No offense is taken, sir. I would much rather understand expectations in advance." Mrs. Gardiner sipped her tea.

How different they were to the Matlocks, gracious and pleasant, looking to be pleased, not offended.

Mr. Gardiner set his teacup aside and crossed his legs. "Now, you said something about spaniels, or was it pointers? You keep a pack of hunting dogs?"

"Indeed I do. I am very fond of spaniels."

"As am I. I would be very interested in seeing your kennel, if I might."

"It would be my pleasure."

Conversation with the Gardiners was easy and agreeable. Their enthusiasm and interest in those things which interested him made what was usually a trial, a delight. When they made their way upstairs, he felt the loss of their company severely. At least dinner tonight would be a far more pleasing event.

If only Elizabeth might join them as well.

The Gardiners arrived in the drawing room in dinner dress. Darcy and Fitzwilliam greeted them.

"A pleasure to make your acquaintance, Colonel Fitzwilliam." Mrs. Gardiner curtsied.

"Indeed, our niece has told us a great deal about you." Mr. Gardiner winked.

Fitzwilliam laughed. "That may or may not be a good thing."

"Well, in this case, you may be certain it is good."

The Gardiners' manners would be welcome in any society drawing room, much more so than the Matlocks'. How strange that there had been a time he was set against them.

"My parents send their regrets tonight as neither will be joining us for dinner."

Darcy grumbled under his breath.

"It is not my fault, Darce. Father complains his gout is making him miserable. Given he has been at the port to ease his discomfort, it is just as well not to have his company. Mother's headaches continue, as does her supply of the good surgeon's tonic."

How very convenient that their ailments enabled them to make their opinions known, with no tarnish to their own reputations. Darcy squeezed his temples.

"So then it will be a small, intimate dinner. The kind we most enjoy," Mrs. Gardiner said.

Was she always so able to see the pleasing aspects in everything? Perhaps Elizabeth learned the skill from her.

"It is a shame to take up the entire dining room for just the four of us." Fitzwilliam rubbed his knuckles along his jaw. "What say you of shifting us to the small dining parlor? I will invite Georgiana to join us. We shall have a merry little party."

Darcy glanced at the Gardiners. Would it insult them, to be treated so familiarly?

"What a lovely idea. There is never so much good conversation as when the table is small and the company amiable," Mrs. Gardiner said.

Fitzwilliam sauntered off to inform Mrs. Reynolds and fetch Georgiana.

In less than a quarter hour, they assembled in the small dining room, the room he and Elizabeth favored. Mirrors glinted from three of the walls, reflecting the candle light and offering an illusion of space. Still, it was confining with barely enough room to skirt around the table, so no servants could attend them. Then again, that was perhaps the room's chiefest appeal. The sense of closeness to the other diners and lack of interruption from the staff made it much easier to converse and enjoy the meal.

The small table would not accommodate all the dishes planned for the evening.

Bless Mrs. Reynolds! She edited the selection to those Elizabeth would have chosen, not Lady Matlock. How delightful not to have to pretend he liked the Fitzwilliam carrot soup again.

"Elizabeth sets a very fine table, does she not?" Mr. Gardiner said.

"Yes, she does," Georgiana whispered, not looking up from her plate.

"That is perhaps the one way she takes after her mother. Fanny is an excellent hostess. She learned from the best, my niece did."

"Have you enjoyed having a sister in the house? I am sure it is a big change for you." Mrs. Gardiner asked.

"Yes, it has been a big change. Since my father passed, we have entertained very little for the holiday, hardly at all. It has been very different trying to plan a ball."

"A ball?"

Darcy glared at Georgiana. What was she about, mentioning that?

"Unfortunately, we had to cancel it with Mrs. Darcy's injury. There is no way she can carry off such an event whilst she is still unable to walk downstairs."

"It is sad that you had to withdraw the invitation. I know she must be disappointed." Mrs. Gardiner chewed her lip. "I remember when I was a girl, living in Lambton, invitations to events at Pemberley were much anticipated. Of course, we were not on such terms to be invited to formal events, like a ball. One year, though, there was a summer picnic for all the children on Pemberley grounds."

Fitzwilliam scratched his head. "Yes, yes, I think I recall that. I was barely breeched at the time."

"I believe the event was in honor of Mr. Darcy's breeching as a matter of fact." Mrs. Gardiner giggled.

Georgiana tittered. "I have never imagined you in a baby dress, brother."

"Then you have been ignoring the portrait in the gallery?" Fitzwilliam served himself another helping of medlars with walnuts.

"I totally forgot about that picture. Your curls were so lovely, brother. It is a shame they were all cut off."

Darcy grumbled. "I was too young to clearly recall the event."

He would protest her informality, but it was so pleasing to see her returned to conversation and participation that he dare not remark on it. She was far too sensitive to anything resembling criticism. Perhaps Elizabeth could teach her to be more resilient.

"You can be assured that it was a lovely event, with games of all sorts for the children, some lovely refreshments, and plenty of biscuits. I remember taking home a lovely little box of pretty biscuits. I think Mrs. Darcy herself folded it for the occasion. I may even still have it … indeed I do. I keep locks of my sons' hair from their breechings in that box."

"What a very sweet thing to do!" Georgiana exclaimed. "Elizabeth talked of hosting a picnic for the children instead of inviting them to the ball."

"A Christmas picnic for the children. What a lovely idea. What date for it?"

"There is no date, not now." Georgiana shrugged.

"I thought you were planning that." Fitzwilliam leaned forward on his elbows. "I do not recalling hearing you had cancelled it as well, Darcy."

Georgiana swallowed hard. "I … I told Elizabeth … I could not …"

"She never mentioned it to me." Darcy steepled his hands. "The picnic invitations were sent along with the ones to the ball, but the only ones I rescinded were for the ball."

"It would seem we have a problem." Fitzwilliam laced his fingers and tapped his thumbs. "I do not relish the thought of packs of expectant children and their parents arriving on the grounds with nothing to greet them."

"You must tell everyone it is canceled, brother. We cannot possible manage … I cannot …" Georgina flapped her hands like a nervous hen.

"I am reluctant to withdraw yet another invitation."

"It would look rather badly on the estate," Mr. Gardiner nodded slowly, forehead drawn tight. "Such things can reflect poorly on the family, I am afraid. Children can be most unforgiving of disappointment."

"Have any preparations been made?" Mrs. Gardiner looked squarely at Georgiana.

"Elizabeth and I spoke with Mrs. Reynolds and Cook about refreshments and biscuits. Supplies may have been ordered, but I do not know for certain." Georgiana squirmed and stared at the table.

"Then there is very little problem at all." Mrs. Gardiner tapped the table.

"What do you mean?" Georgiana asked.

"With the Darcys' permission, I would be happy to assist you. Planning a picnic is not so very difficult. I am certain we can make the necessary arrangements and welcome the children and their parents for several hours of good fun without taxing anyone's good nature."

"I do not think it a good idea." Georgiana pushed her chair back from the table.

"I think it is a splendid notion and a very generous one of you, Mrs. Gardiner." Fitzwilliam lifted an eyebrow toward Georgiana.

"I do not think it a good plan at all. Aunt Matlock is so opposed to the idea. She will be—"

"She does not like anything that she did not propose herself. She will bluster and worry, but in the end, this is Pemberley, not Matlock, and the Darcys, not the Matlocks must be pleased." Fitzwilliam lifted his glass in a toast.

"Well said, Colonel." Mr. Gardiner raised his glass to match. "What say you, Darcy?"

"Elizabeth esteems you very greatly. I know she will be very pleased for your assistance."

He did not have an opportunity to bring the matter to her attention that night, though. She slept, though fitfully, when he arrived in their chambers. Best not wake her. The good news could wait until the morrow.

The next morning, Elizabeth lay awake, but eyes closed, listening to Darcy's morning preparations. She had been awake when he slipped out of bed and padded into the dressing room. His valet was as quiet as he. Only hushed words passed between them during his ablutions. Then he slipped out of the door, just as quietly.

The door latch clicked, and she sat up.

Perhaps she should have risen with him, but why invite another demonstration of his displeasure? After he left her in the gallery with nary a word, how could she expect anything else?

She swung her legs over the edge of the bed. Her ankle throbbed with the effort, but the pain was finally subsiding. Though the walking sticks were clumsy and uncomfortable, they did help. Getting out of her room was good, but being able to get downstairs would be better.

Perhaps in a few more days, she would be able to enlist the help of the footmen in getting downstairs, at least once a day.

How pleasing it would be to be able to …

To what? To sit at the dining table to meals she did not order? To meet with Mrs. Reynolds, knowing her efforts made no difference at all to the running of the estate? To discover her presence or absence made little impact?

She slumped and caught herself with her hands. Perhaps it was better to keep to herself after all.

But no, the Gardiners had arrived yesterday. Darcy whispered something about that when he came into the room to dress for dinner. The laudanum muddled haze in her head made it difficult to recall.

Dash it all!

No more of that tonic, regardless of how her ankle felt. Mrs. Reynolds knew how to brew willow bark. A strong decoction of that had to be a better option than the confusion and the horrid muzzy feeling the laudanum left in its wake.

She must see Aunt Gardiner. She was the embodiment of sunshine and warmth, and with the fire not chasing away enough of the chill, that was exactly what she needed.

Taking up the walking sticks, she hobbled into the dressing room and rang for her maid. The girl must have been waiting with bated breath for the ring because she seemed to appear instantly.

"Mrs. Gardiner has asked after you, mum, and requests that she might be able to see you when you are well enough." The maid pinned her hair.

"After I am dressed, and a tray with tea and toast is sent, tell her I am at her disposal."

The maid disappeared through the servant's door.

Had she been able, Elizabeth would have paced the room. Instead, all the energy built within, itchy and twitchy in her limbs.

She shook out her hands. That helped, a little.

A dainty knock sounded from the doorway and the door creaked open. "Lizzy?"

"Aunt!" She pulled up on the walking sticks and made her way halfway across the room.

Aunt Gardiner caught her by the elbow as she lost her balance. "Oh, my dear girl, this was not at all how I expected to see you. Here, pray sit down. You are making me nervous just watching you."

They sat on the small couch near the tea table.

"I have all the grace of a newly born calf, but it is far better than keeping to the fainting couch waiting on someone to carry me to and fro."

"I can only imagine the torture this has been for you."

"Of a very special kind, indeed. I suppose if Mama had ever puzzled out what being kept to a single room does to me, she would have had a far more effective way of managing me."

"How are you faring, Lizzy?"

She turned aside.

"I am worried you know."

"It will be well, you need not be concerned. How are your rooms?"

"We are very pleased with them. I think it most thoughtful you saw us set up in the family wing. We would much rather be closer to you than ensconced in the fine suites, tucked away where no one can see or hear us."

"The family wing?"

"You were not aware?"

"There has been some ... confusion ... as to accommodations ... and after I was hurt ..."

"Then it was Mr. Darcy's consideration. I will certainly thank him. He has been quite solicitous."

"He is most kind."

"Lizzy. There is something you are not telling me. Do not argue. I know your look very well."

Elizabeth fell against the back of the couch, eyes closed. What point in denying it? Aunt would draw the truth out of her sooner or later.

"It is difficult to please him. Managing the household here has been more challenging than I was prepared for."

"What do you mean difficult to please? Pray forgive me, but we saw nothing of the kind at all last night. In fact when Colonel Fitzwilliam suggested we move to the small dining parlor for dinner without his aunt and uncle, he was all accommodations. Even happy for the change."

"I am glad he was pleased with his cousin's suggestions. I fear he has not been so pleased with mine." She clutched her teacup hard.

"He seemed quite content with the Christmas picnic you are planning."

"Picnic? Georgiana was to plan it, but she said that he told her she did not need to do so. I expected it had been canceled with the ball."

"That was not at all the impression I received last night. He seemed quite dissatisfied that she had not been working on it and refused to call it off."

"I am all astonishment."

"I offered to assist in whatever ways I might."

"You?"

"I thought you would be unable, but I am happy to see that I am wrong. I expect you are very disappointed about the ball. But we might still be able to offer some sort of hospitality at the estate."

"I am without words. Truly I do not know what to say. All this is so very different to what I understood. I am pleased by the notion, but very confused."

"My dear, you need to have a conversation with your husband." She peered deeply into Elizabeth's eyes. "You have not been talking very much have you?"

"He has been busy, and I have been indisposed."

Aunt slapped the seat of the couch. "Do not offer such flimsy excuses. I know your headstrong nature. I have seen how overbearing he can be when attempting to care for those he loves. That is not a combination apt to produce peace. Truly, you must swallow your pride and talk to him. I believe you will be surprised at what you hear."

"In truth, I dread what I will hear. I am certain he will be quite displeased with me. I am not used to that, at least from anyone but Mama. I … I do not like inviting censure."

"None of us do. But, marriage is not for cowards. You must fortify yourself and discuss these matters with him. I am certain there have been substantial misunderstandins all around."

Elizabeth shrugged. "I suppose that is possible. I will consider what you say."

"Good girl. Now, your delightful Mrs. Reynolds has helped me gather all the notes that have been made regarding the picnic. I thought you would like to go over them with me and see what there is yet to do."

Aunt Gardiner was right; it felt good to be useful again. And perhaps, since Aunt and Georgiana were involved, Darcy would not feel the need to correct all her planning once again.

Darcy sat in his study, examining a neatly penciled list. Elizabeth's handwriting was nearly as pleasant as her voice, and had been all he had heard from her in days now. Sharing the same room with her should have ensured they would talk, but he heard barely more now than before.

Her aunt seemed encouraging though. She delivered the list into his hands, assuring him planning the picnic had much improved Elizabeth's spirits.

Should he tell her he would much rather stage the picnic than the ball? It was far more agreeable to him to be able to mingle amongst his farmers—who would inevitably accompany their children on an outing at the manor—and discuss the fields and flocks over a pint of cider than to wander about in fine clothing, wondering whom he would offend next.

Yes, this was a splendid plan indeed. No doubt she understood that though.

In the spring, they could have a ball, if she wished.

Stomping and swishing of skirts preceded an unladylike pounding at his door. "Darcy!"

He dropped the list and threw his head back into the chair. "Enter."

Aunt Matlock stormed inside, a rustling mass of silk and temper. She planted herself before his desk, arms folded over her chest.

"What may I do for you?" Darcy rose to his feet. How convenient that he might tower over her this way. She needed the reminder this was not her domain to rule.

"What is the meaning of this?"

"What are you talking about?"

Perhaps Fitzwilliam was right; she was going a bit daft.

"I heard the kitchen talking about baking biscuits for a picnic."

What was she doing in the kitchen?

"What of it. They have their assignment. I do not see why it is any matter to you."

"I thought that nonsense had been finally put to rest. You cancelled the ball; you cancelled everything. Just as you should have. All of these ill-conceived notions to entertain this season, you put them to rest."

"You misunderstood. Surely Elizabeth cannot manage a ball in her condition, however, the picnic, with the help of her aunt—"

"That woman? You would have her help planning, but not mine? She is in trade!"

"I believe it is her husband who is in trade."

"Do not get smart with me, young man. They are in trade. What do they know of society or how to manage … anything?"

Far more than Matlock whose debts grew faster than the estate's income.

"Why is that of any concern to you?"

"The Darcy name? The reputation of Pemberley? Is that not of any matter to you?"

"Of course it is."

"Then why do you insist upon tarnishing it with events planned without proper—"

"Proper what?"

"What does your country hoyden know about society events?"

"A picnic for children is hardly a society event."

"The parents will attend."

"The guests are the residents of Pemberley. I do not think that qualifies as the height of fashionable society."

"Exactly my point. It is abhorrent that the first time you entertain, you snub those of your quality in favor of … of … the lower classes. I told you, Lady Catherine and I both told you, this is what would happen. The quiet denigration of Pemberley's standing. Vulgar mushrooms springing up in the shade of an ancient and noble family. And you seem happy to aid and abet them. How can you?"

"Vulgar mushrooms? Are you referring to my wife or my tenants? Neither is an acceptable analogy I assure you. I just prefer to recognize the level to which I have been insulted before I make my reply." Darcy clenched his fists behind his back.

She drove her index finger into his chest. "You have been insulted? What of us? Do you not comprehend how very disagreeable it is to be given bad connections when one is not accustomed to them?"

"What bad connections?"

"That uncle in trade. I find it insulting to be tied to such."

"At least he pays his debts. He has not collectors hounding his door. I dare say, neither he nor his family have ever had the threat of debtor's prison held over their heads. I cannot say the same for you."

"Do not discuss the Viscount. That is no matter of yours and has nothing to do—"

"It has everything to do with this! You declare her connections ridiculous and disagreeable. In truth, I do not have to look nearly so far to find disagreeable and ignoble connections; sufficient reside in my own family for both of us. I should thank her for being willing to take on my connections and sully herself with them."

Oh, Aunt Matlock did not like that at all.

Her voice dropped to a trembling whisper. "This is not to be borne, I tell you. I will not be insulted in this manner."

"You brought it on yourself, madam. Recall, I am not the one who sought you out, demanding you manage your family according to my standards."

"Insolent, impudent boy!"

"I beg you to recall, I am not a boy, madam. I am Master of this estate and you are a guest in my house."

"A dubious honor at best."

"One that you need not have imposed upon yourself."

"Is that a threat?"

"I do not make threats. It is simply an option that is open to you."

But he could make it a threat if it would help.

"How dare you! I know how to act. I will, I will, do not mistake me. I will."

"Then be about it quickly. My staff, and I dare say my wife, have been sufficiently inconvenienced by you. They need not endure anymore." He pointed toward the door.

She turned crimson and sputtered, stamped and huffed.

He sat at his desk and raised the list before his face.

She stomped out and slammed the door behind her.

Heavens what had he done?

Mother would be … would she be upset, or would she be proud he had stood up to Aunt Matlock? It was not as if she and Mother ever got along very well to begin with. At the very least, Mother would have laughed at the show of temper to which Lady Matlock had been reduced in the hopes of getting her way.

Had she seen, Elizabeth would probably have been amused, if a touch mortified, as well. Perhaps tonight they might share a laugh over it all.

First though, he must return the list to Mrs. Reynolds. They would need more beer and cider. The ladies probably did not anticipate the number of farmers who would happily enjoy the event with their families.

Elizabeth relaxed in the small sitting room, reading Lady Anne's fond memories of Darcy's breeching and the picnic that followed. Her journal included a small folded envelope containing a lock of his hair, cut in honor of the event. Two little sketches accompanied it. Young Darcy's profile before and after. The starched, frilled collar of his new skeleton suit must have itched along his neck where his mass of curly locks had been shorn.

He had been a very handsome boy. Not cute, handsome. Even then, he carried a serious dignity about him.

Mrs. Reynolds burst in. "Mrs. Darcy! Mrs. Darcy! There has been such a to-do!"

Elizabeth reached for her walking sticks. "What has happened? Is something wrong with one of the children?"

"Heavens no, it is far worse. The Lady Matlock ordered all their trunks packed immediately. They are departing even as we speak."

"Departing? What happened?"

"I do not fully know, madam, but I heard such goings on from the master's study. I fear they have had a great falling out."

"What did they argued about?"

"I believe I heard the Christmas picnic spoken of in very loud tones."

No doubt Lady Matlock objected to Aunt Gardiner's involvement when she herself had been refused the honor.

"I must go downstairs and deal with this immediately."

"You cannot manage the steps."

"Call for the two strongest footmen. I will be downstairs if I must crawl there. I would prefer not to, but make no mistake, I will not be dissuaded."

"Yes, madam." Mrs. Reynolds curtsied and ran out.

Elizabeth closed the journal carefully and heaved herself up. She tottered to the top of the stairs where two footmen and Mrs. Reynolds met her.

"Carefully, carefully!" she cried as she took Elizabeth's walking sticks.

The two men linked their arms and formed a chair of sorts and Elizabeth sat down. She slipped her arms over their shoulders. They began their decent, Mrs. Reynolds calling directions from behind them.

Below, Lady Matlock screeched orders at the scrambling staff. Her own maid and Lord Matlock's valet stood with her, issuing their own instructions to their juniors. They turned to look at the odd parade down the stairs and the screeching stopped.

The footmen set her down ever so gently, holding her arms until she arranged the walking stick to bear her weight.

"You! You! This is your fault. You are a disgrace to this noble home and a disgrace to your family. You do not deserve to bear the name of Darcy. He should have set you up under his protection, if he had to have you, and established a proper mistress in this house." She pointed, her hands shaking.

"Mrs. Reynolds, direct the staff to their duties. We will be in the parlor."

"I am going nowhere with you! You are an affront … a … an embarrassment …"

"Elizabeth!" Darcy rushed to her side. "What are you doing here? How did you get downstairs?"

"I heard the commotion. Pray come, Lady Matlock. We might discuss—"

"I have no desire to have any kind of a discussion with any of you."

Aunt Gardiner glided down the steps and stopped beside Lady Matlock. "Not all discussions are calm or comfortable, but no doubt a woman of your station comprehends the need for a family to settle the inevitable little disagreements in a private, civilized fashion. Elizabeth?"

"Indeed, pray join us. Mrs. Reynolds, send a tea tray."

"Yes, madam." Mrs. Reynolds clearly fought back a smile.

Several young maids hung close to the walls, straining to hear the conversation. No doubt they would be the center of much conversation below stairs tonight.

Aunt Gardiner stood close, ready to catch her if she lost her balance. Darcy took up the other side. They slowly paraded to the parlor, Lady Matlock quietly fuming behind them.

Darcy shut the door.

Lady Matlock strutted around the room, as if surveying her territory. But the room was designed to suit Lady Anne, not her, and she did not settle easily. She peeked at the shelf of bric-a-brac, surveyed the bookcase, and finally came to rest on the soft couch near the middle of room. Perhaps she intended to hold court.

"Now that we have a modicum of privacy, perhaps the discussion may continue in a more polite fashion." Aunt Gardiner sat near Lady Matlock.

"I will not stay here to watch my nephew make a fool of himself and his family as he revels in his low connections."

Elizabeth's hand shook so hard, she almost lost grip on her walking sticks, but Aunt Gardiner did not even blink. How did she do it?

"And I will not harbor a woman with such clear designs against those under my protection." Darcy stomped toward them.

"Designs? Stop speaking nonsense!"

"You are the threatening to promise my sister to the son of a Scottish lord and send my wife—"

Elizabeth's jaw dropped.

So did Lady Matlock's. "What nonsense are you blathering about?"

"Georgiana said your last letter—"

"My last letter made mention that a Miss Milken of our acquaintance has been engaged to a Scottish lord. I merely noted Georgiana should be so lucky as to secure such a marriage."

Darcy's brow knotted and he leaned back. "You were not contriving to send my wife to Scotland?"

"I may not approve of your choice, Darcy, but that is below me. Entirely disgraceful."

"Pray Aunt, would you fetch Georgiana to us?" Elizabeth fought to keep her voice soft and even.

"Indeed, I would hear it from her own mouth." Lady Matlock crossed her arms and glowered.

Aunt slipped out. If anyone could manage a sullen girl, it was her.

Darcy edged a little closer to Elizabeth. "Pray, would it not be better for you to sit down? It would not be profitable for you to overtax yourself."

Darcy brought a chair toward her and helped her sit. He placed the walking sticks just out of reach.

She raised an eyebrow toward him.

"I will assist you when you wish to rise again."

He had that look of determination in his eye, the one there was little point in arguing with.

Aunt Gardiner returned, holding an ashen Georgiana's elbow, and presented her to Darcy.

Darcy stood just behind Elizabeth and cleared his throat.

"Georgiana, there are some things which we must discuss." Elizabeth cut him off. "Tell us of your Aunt Matlock's most recent letter."

She covered her mouth and stammered something clearly not intended to be understood.

"What did you tell him I wrote?" Lady Matlock stomped to stand nose to nose with Georgiana.

"I … I … that is …"

"That I would marry you off to some Scot, sight unseen? That I was willing to send her away with you? Falsehoods? That is entirely below you. It is disgraceful, utterly disgraceful!"

"But, I, that is not what I said, not what I meant."

Darcy stood beside Lady Matlock. "It is precisely what you told me, Georgiana. Precisely."

"But that is not what I meant!"

"What else could you have meant? No, you intentionally misled me, but I cannot understand to what purpose."

"Pray, do not be angry with me. I did not mean that you should believe—"

"Stop it." Elizabeth said sharply. "This is not the behavior we expect of a girl nearly grown. Certainly not one of your standing. If your word cannot be trusted, then we have failed—"

"I have failed." Darcy glowered, a truly frightening expression. "I have failed in raising you. When did you learn to lie? How long have you been lying to me?"

"All you do is criticize me!" Georgiana pumped her fists at her sides. "And remind me of every mistake I have made. I am so tired of being told I have disappointed all of you, of how I am unworthy and do not deserve the kindness I have been shown."

"Neither your brother nor I say those things to you. I am coming to doubt that your Aunt is as apt repeat those things either."

"But … but …" she turned in a little circle, as though trying to see all of them at once.

"It is painful to be reminded of our failings, to be sure. But there has been no shortage of grace offered you. It would seem either you do not believe you have been forgiven or do not believe that what you have done is so overwhelmingly bad as to have earned you such censure. Or perhaps you do not wish to change. In any case, humility is necessary for all of us, especially for a lady."

"I said I am sorry. What do you want of me?" She stamped softly.

"To stop behaving like a petulant little girl," Aunt Matlock said.

"I am not."

"Yes you are. I had first thought Lady Matlock too harsh when she said that of you, but I confess I was wrong and she was right. And Lady Matlock, I apologize to you for disbelieving you on the matter."

Lady Matlock blinked several times.

"You see, you are criticizing me." Georgiana sniffled and dragged the back of her hand across her eyes.

"Stop it right now. I have three younger sisters and I well recognize what you are doing. We will have no more of it. I shall inform Mrs. Annesley to correct such behavior in the future."

"You are not going to let her speak to me like this, are you brother?"

Darcy raised his hands and extended them to Elizabeth. "She is mistress of this house and I defer to her regarding the children of the household."

"I am not a child."

"You are acting like one and will be treated like one until you prove to us otherwise." From the corner of her eye, Elizabeth caught Darcy's nod. "To do so, you must stop hiding in your room and fulfill your duties and responsibilities. I will not have you continuing to shirk what is required of you."

"You will begin immediately." Darcy cut Georgiana off before she could protest. "No more meals in your room. If you do not wish to join us, you will not have a tray sent to you."

Elizabeth pushed up on the arms of the chair. Darcy handed her the walking sticks.

"Your brother is quite correct. Be sure we will deal with the issue of your falsehoods later, and you will face punishment for those as well. Go to your room and think about what you have done and what would be an appropriate penance for you to offer for your behavior. You are dismissed, Georgiana."

"No, that is not fair."

"I quite agree. That is entirely fitting." Lady Matlock moved to Elizabeth's side.

"Come with me," Aunt Gardiner took Georgiana's elbow and half-led, half-dragged her away.

Lady Matlock sniffed. "I must say, Mrs. Darcy, growing up with four sisters seems to have given you a way with dealing with young ladies. Perhaps you will be to Georgiana's benefit after all."

"Thank you, Lady Matlock."

"I hardly know what to make of her right now." Darcy raked his fingers through his hair.

"I fear we have not discovered the end of her falsehoods. I must ask you, sir," Elizabeth looked up at Darcy. "Did you give Georgiana permission to leave off planning the picnic or that she could keep to her room entirely?"

"Not at all. She was extremely unsettled by," he turned to his aunt, "your very unexpected arrival. I gave her leave to keep to her room on that day but no more."

Lady Matlock huffed and ruffled her feathers.

"When she took to keeping to her rooms after that, I knew not what to do."

"I see." Elizabeth looked at her hands. "I have been operating under a number of misunderstandings."

Darcy looked at her, eyes wide. "I believe we need a moment, Aunt, if you please."

Lady Matlock muttered under her breath, but left.

Chapter 7

Darcy and Elizabeth stared at each other. He helped her to the couch and sat with her.

She sat very straight and stared at her hands. He reached for her hand.

Pray, let her not pull it away.

"Elizabeth, I fear that there are a great many misunderstandings between us right now."

"I … I believe you are quite correct."

"Fitzwilliam brought it to my attention, that mayhap I offended you with the orders I gave the staff regarding my aunt and uncle's visit."

"It is your house and your family. It is your right to do here as you see fit."

"I failed to consider your decisions and your efforts, taking charge of what was your responsibility."

She shrugged and turned away.

"Pray, look at me."

"I cannot."

"I have hurt you."

"I am sorry I have disappointed you. I will improve. I have been studying, and I will make you proud as a proper mistress of your estate. I am sorry that I have ... have failed in my early attempts, but pray, do not lose faith in me. I will ..." Her voice cracked.

He gripped her hand tightly. "How could you think such a thing of me?"

"You say so little, I understand you by your actions. What else was I to believe when you ordered menus changed and rooms rearranged, and it seemed you disregarded my instructions to Georgiana?"

"You might have believed my aunt's arrival sent me into a panic."

"I have never known you to panic, much less at something so trivial as the arrival of guests."

"Uncle and Aunt Matlock are hardly typical or trivial guests."

She snickered. Was he trying to be humorous? The sincerity in his eyes suggested not.

"I have never had a proper mistress in my home until now. The staff has always turned to me in such situations. I began handing out instructions without recalling that there was another, far better qualified than myself to deal with the matter."

"But I am not."

"Yes, you are. I might know my family's preferences, but you are far better equipped to manage the household and my sister. I should have considered that, and consulted with you on the matters."

"I would have given way to your preferences. It all would have turned out the same. What difference how we get to that place?"

"You would not have spent these weeks avoiding me and not speaking to me. Worse, I fear your injury is the result of—"

"Of my foolishness, sir. My own foolishness."

"You are no fool, Elizabeth." He caressed the crest of her cheek with his fingertips.

She leaned into his touch. How long had it been since she had done so?

"Yes, I am. I should have come to you with my grievances. I allowed my pride to govern my reactions. You are no ogre. I was far too ready to believe I knew your thoughts and feelings on the matter. It all seemed so obvious—and so wrong."

"I am sorry it is easy to believe so badly of me." He cradled her cheek in his palm and caught a hot trickle with his thumb.

"I am ashamed I thought as I did. You have proven yourself a better man than that." She laid her hand over his. "I suppose Georgiana is not the only one who needs to learn a bit of humility."

"I did little better. I was so entrenched in my own habits. I never stopped to think about how things are different now, how they must be different. I over-stepped myself, and I am most heartily sorry."

"I, too."

"Do you have any idea how I missed you those days you locked yourself in your room? Pray, do not ever do that to me again."

"I did not enjoy it either. I have been so very lonely."

"As have I." He pressed his forehead to hers. "I fear, I do not do very well on my own any more. Do not leave me to myself, Elizabeth, I need you."

"I was miserable, thinking I had disappointed you, when all I desire is to make you proud, and happy that you married as you did."

"I am and always will be."

She closed her eyes and leaned into him, warm and soft, lips so close to his. Her warmth suffused through him.

What was a man to do with that?

He leaned nearer still, and she closed the gap, meeting in a kiss that began as chaste.

She responded with hunger and longing, deep as his own, drawing from him yearnings almost too powerful to contain.

She did not withdraw, caressing the back of his neck with her fingertips, knotting her hand into his hair.

Had she any idea of what she did to him?

He pulled closer, wrapping his arms around her back, pressing her to him. Her intoxicating scent filled his senses, calming and inflaming him at the same time.

Sharp voices carried from some distant part of the house.

Blast it all! There were guests in the house, and this room was hardly private.

He pulled back just enough to catch his breath and pressed his cheek to hers. "Do not think we are by any means finished. You wish to understand me by my actions. I have every intention of making myself very clearly understood."

She purred against him.

Great heavens! That sound alone might entirely undo him!

"I shall anticipate understanding you much better, soon." Her fingers trailed behind his ear and along the side of his face.

That was not making self-control any easier. Far from it.

He took her hand and kissed each finger. "Now things are as they should be."

"At least some things." She leaned her head into his shoulder.

"The most important one." He kissed the top of her head. "But you are right. What are we to do with Georgiana?"

"She needs a firm hand and guidance. She has become spoilt, the only child between two guardians who frankly dote on her too much. Yes, she is naturally shy and reticent, but it has now gone too far. She is becoming selfish and lazy. Those traits must be nipped immediately before they are become entrenched."

"But she does not deserve to be continually punished—"

"This has nothing to do with Ramsgate. She is using it as an excuse to avoid whatever is inconvenient to her. It must stop. She is, for now, a sweet girl, and I wish to see her continue to be so. She is not so far gone that we cannot help her recover. Perhaps we should invite my sister Kitty to join us for some months. The two of them might benefit one another."

"Indeed?"

"Kitty will have little tolerance for the games Georgiana is playing and will help us curb them. While Georgiana's manners and refinement will demonstrate to Kitty what she is lacking. She will begin to ape a better example than Lydia."

Darcy nodded. "A very good notion to consider for the new year. For now though, what do you think about the picnic? Are you comfortable with your aunt's offer to help us carry it off?"

"I do see the wisdom in not attempting the ball at this time, but I hated to call off everything. Something for the children would make me very happy."

"I, too. Then we shall go forward with it, with or preferably without my aunt's blessings. It will be best to establish now that she does not rule our family, much as you did with Aunt Catherine."

"Must you remind me? I was so rude that day."

"The majority of the rudeness must be credited to her. You will note, though, she has not attempted to manage our lives since that point. I hope that the same shall be true of Aunt Matlock."

Elizabeth sighed. "This was not how I envisioned our first Christmastide together."

"Nor I. But it is hardly over; in fact, it is barely begun."

She cuddled into him.

Oh, yes, it was hardly begun at all.

Several minutes later, Fitzwilliam sauntered in. He looked at them, smiled a suggestive smile and waggled his eyebrows.

"Much better," he murmured as he dragged another chair close to them and fell into it.

"I imagine you came for a reason?"

Subtlety had never been Fitzwilliam's strong suit.

"I thought it would be amusing to watch the two of you. You know the estate is utterly lacking in any other form of entertainment."

"Had I known, I would have brought riddles for charades." Elizabeth cocked her head, her eyebrow lifting just so.

Fitzwilliam snickered. "I am also sent to inform you my mother intends to depart immediately. She cannot

not conscience the picnic you are planning and will not offer an honorable surrender on the matter."

"I am sorry—"

Darcy tightened his arm around her. "Do not be. She was not invited and did not bother to even announce her visit. She probably hopes we will grovel and beg her to stay. I do not regret her leaving."

Fitzwilliam cleared his throat.

"No offense to you, cousin."

"None taken, I am sure. However, I would like to ask a favor of you, Mrs. Darcy." He bowed from his shoulders.

"Certainly, what can we do for you?" Elizabeth said before Darcy could release the snide remark on the tip of his tongue.

"I know I have not been invited, but I would covet an invitation for the holiday."

Elizabeth glanced at Darcy and they shared a nod.

"You, sir, are a most welcome guest. Pray, just tell me the room you favor and your favorite foods, and you will be welcome at any time."

A smile, a genuine one, broad and toothy, but tinged with an air of sadness, lit his face. "And to what do I owe such an honor?"

"I expect my wife considers you the most sensible of my relations."

"I am not sure if that is a compliment or a condemnation, madam, but I appreciate your hospitality nonetheless."

Lord and Lady Matlock visited her in the parlor for a take leave. It was the least they could do for the hospitality—and patience—she had extended.

They did not go so far as to apologize for the slights to their hostess, but they hinted, and only hinted, that their visit might, possibly, in some lights, be regarded as poorly timed and inconvenient. From most, the sentiments would have been hardly acceptable, but from the Matlocks, it was groveling. Just as surprising, they graciously received Elizabeth's apologies for the misunderstandings stemming from Georgiana's deceit. All in all, their departure was as peaceful as one might hope it could be.

Dinner was served in the small dining room. Since Elizabeth could not make it upstairs to change, Darcy insisted on an informal event and required Georgiana to join them. The menu reflected Elizabeth's tastes, not the Matlocks'.

How had Mrs. Reynolds surmised the Matlocks would not be joining them for dinner? She was indeed a treasure.

Good humor and excellent conversation, if at moments a tad improper, reigned, thanks to Fitzwilliam. Thankfully, the Gardiners' sense of humor appreciated the unpolished soldier's wit.

In the correct company, it was not nearly so difficult to talk as Darcy had always found it to be. Clearly, Elizabeth was the correct company.

They adjourned together for the drawing room, at Elizabeth's suggestion.

After an evening of word games and a round of commerce, they all retired.

Darcy supervised the footmen carrying Elizabeth back up the stairs. He grumbled and murmured to himself the entire way.

They set her down three steps from the top of the staircase and hurried away at Darcy's dismissal. No doubt his scrutiny made them as uncomfortable as he. He helped her arrange her walking sticks.

"I am sorry you do not like that," she whispered.

"No, I do not. I do not find it proper that they should have their hands on your person."

"It is not entirely comfortable for me either. Does that make you feel any better?"

"Yes." He dragged the toe of one boot along the carpet.

"Would you be willing to permit me their help? I feel better for being able to be downstairs some of the day."

"Might I carry you instead?"

"It is not safe for you to do so alone. It would not do for both of us to fall. But … what if we asked Fitzwilliam for his assistance to carry me down as the footmen did? Would that be acceptable?"

Darcy sighed. "Fitzwilliam is family to us. That must be better than the servants."

"Then I suppose it is a good thing he is extending his stay with us, is it not?"

"I knew he would have to prove himself good for something sooner or later."

He held the door of their dressing room for her. Her lady's maid waited inside.

"I will be in our room in a moment." She smiled at him.

Everything in him went warm and fuzzy in the light of her smile.

How long had he been denied it? Probably only a fortnight, but it felt far, far longer.

His valet helped him undress, and he sat on the edge of the bed waiting, a single candle lit. The mantle clock ticked, marking slow seconds, tempting him to barge into the dressing room to make certain she was still coming to join him.

The dressing room door swung open.

"You are beautiful, Mrs. Darcy."

She slid onto the bed beside him. "Thank you, sir."

He slid close and wrapped his arm around her waist. "I thought perhaps I might read to you tonight."

"Read to me? That is something new. I think I should enjoy it. You have an excellent reading voice, sir." She leaned into his shoulder and peered at the text in his hand.

"I trust you will enjoy some poetry."

"Oh, poetry. You have become rather reflective, have you not?"

"I would not call this reflective." His brushed his fingers over a stanza.

Elizabeth sucked in a breath.

The sound sent shivers coursing down his spine. Had she any idea what she did to him?

He cast a sidelong glance at her.

She knew.

She knew very well. And she seemed to enjoy it.

He laid aside the book and blew out the candle. Some poetry needed no words.

Elizabeth sat in the upstairs sitting room, reading. Now things were returned to normal, a few minutes on her own proved pleasant, not isolating. Earlier that day, Darcy and Fitzwilliam had taken the children and Georgiana to cut decorations for the house. Evergreen boughs and Christmas roses adorned the mantle and filled vases on the tables throughout the house, the fruits of those labors.

What a change a few days and an alteration in company made. Though there had been a few frenzied moments in planning, all in all, peace had returned and with it a sense of the Christmastide season.

Mrs. Reynolds peeked into the room. "It is almost here, madam. The Pemberley tradition is for the family to gather in the parlor."

Darcy and Fitzwilliam arrived a moment later.

"Come, my lady, your chariot waits." Fitzwilliam bowed.

"I am quite capable in getting to the stairs on my own. I have become quite handy with these walking sticks now. Perhaps I might suggest them as a new fashionable accessory for the *ton*."

Fitzwilliam sniggered. "Do not say that too loudly. All it would take is one of Almack's patronesses to appear in company with them. The next day everyone will be clamoring for them. You might speak to Bingley. There could be a fortune to be made in selling fashionable walking sticks to ladies."

Darcy snickered.

Oh, how lovely it was to hear him in good humor once again. The house was glum and dreary without his laughter.

They carried her downstairs to the parlor where the Gardiners awaited.

Soon she would attempt the stairs on her own. The novelty in being carried had worn off. She longed for the freedom to come and go as she pleased. Darcy, though, would probably regret the loss of the excuse to be so close to her in public. She would miss that, too.

The fragrance of evergreens enveloped them, the room bearing a veritable forest of boughs, decked with gay red and white ribbons. Mama decorated this way too. More than anything, this brought the feelings of the Yuletide season to life.

Georgiana pressed her nose to the glass. "I see them coming!"

The children crowded around her. They had never seen a Yule log before. In town, the Gardiners celebrated with a Yule candle.

"Is the hot cider ready?" Elizabeth asked.

"Yes, madam, and there is bread and cheese in the kitchen for the men," Mrs. Reynolds answered as she walked past the parlor door.

Elizabeth craned her neck to see out the window. A team of horses and several farmers, trundled up to the front of the house, a huge log chained to the team.

The front door groaned open and clanking chains and men's voices filled the ground floor.

Elizabeth sat on the couch farthest from the door and gathered the children to her. They pressed close, eyes wide at the sight of the men wrestling the enormous log up to the fireplace.

Surely it would not fit. No, there was simply no way.

The children gasped and applauded.

How had they made it fit?

Darcy smiled at her from the other side of the room. He had promised her it would fit and was gloating in the glory of being right.

Dear man.

Darcy and Fitzwilliam thanked the men for their efforts, and Sampson ushered them back to the kitchen for an ample measure of Pemberley's hospitality.

"That is the biggest Yule log I have ever seen," Aunt Gardiner beckoned the children closer to the fireplace.

"Where did it come from, sir?" Matthew, the oldest, tugged Darcy's coat sleeve.

Darcy hunkered down beside him. What an excellent father he would make.

"We have a cooper on the estate. The Yule log has always come from there. It is a log not suitable to his purposes, made a gift, suitable to ours."

"Surely it is large enough to smolder until Twelfth Night," Elizabeth said.

"That is the plan," Darcy said. "Each year, it is the job of the youngest hall boy to sleep in the parlor from Christmas Eve until Twelfth Night. He tends the Yule fire and ensures it remains lit until throughout."

"Do not fear, madam, the lad is well rewarded for his efforts, with all the apples he can roast and toast and cheese he can stuff himself with." Fitzwilliam winked.

Elizabeth giggled.

Darcy waved them all close to the fireplace. He opened a silver box on the mantle and removed two crystal bottles and a silver box. He anointed the log with oil, wine and salt.

"May the fire of this log warm the cold; may the hungry be fed; may the weary find rest and may all enjoy heaven's peace."

He opened a second silver box and extended it toward them. "This is what remains of the last Yule log."

Ashes filled the box. Along one side lay a long splinter.

"Fitzwilliam, would you care to light the log?"

Fitzwilliam rubbed his hands together briskly. "Afraid that you might not be able to manage to start it on the first try yourself, old man?"

Darcy snorted, but held his peace.

Elizabeth snickered.

How like boys they were. But it was good. Fitzwilliam brought out a youthful, almost playful side in Darcy, one that needed release far more often. True, it was a mite prickly, but that could be shaped and softened with time and practice.

Fitzwilliam hunkered down beside the Yule log. Shadows drifted across his face. He stiffened and stared into the fireplace.

Darcy crouched beside him. "Are you well? Should I not have asked you to do this?"

Fitzwilliam swallowed hard and worked at words. "I … I … I can do this." His hands shook

"Let us do it together." Darcy moved close beside him and whispered to Fitzwilliam.

Elizabeth closed her eyes to listen better. He was reminding Fitzwilliam of boyhood times. Times spent in their hunting lodge, of Yule logs past. Of pleasant, peaceful things.

Slowly the trembling stopped, and Fitzwilliam began to breathe more normally.

Together, they struck the spark and fanned it into life. They lit the splinter and nursed the burgeoning blaze until the log burned, too.

Darcy stood and arranged the group around Elizabeth. He extended his hand toward her, and they joined hands in a circle.

"Let us consider the year past. Our faults, mistakes and bad choices. Let us allow the flames to consume those that we may begin the coming year with a clean slate. With that as our starting place, let us purpose to improve our faults, correct our mistakes and make improved choices."

He squeezed her hand hard and peeked at her from the corner of his eyes. She squeezed his hand back.

This was a tradition different to her family's. But it was very pleasing and she would look forward to it in the coming years.

They lingered a moment longer then released the circle.

A pair of maids entered bearing trays of cider, apples for roasting, bread and cheese for toasting.

Darcy tossed Fitzwilliam an apple. "You may have the honors of tending the roasting apples."

Fitzwilliam bit into it instead. Darcy laughed heartily.

Yes, this was the sound to launch a proper Yuletide upon.

The next day, Christmas morning, Darcy called the carriage to take them to church. The picturesque weather made it a shame not to walk with the rest of the family. Even with the walking sticks, she could not have made it there on foot.

Fitzwilliam insisted on walking with Georgiana and the Gardiners. She would miss his sharp wit. But gratitude was a more appropriate sentiment for Christmas morning than jealousy, so she settled back into the seat and leaned against Darcy's shoulder.

He cut a fine figure when he was driving, one worth watching. He glanced at her and winked.

Cheeky man, he knew it too. And seemed to enjoy it as well.

A crowd had already gathered at the church when they arrived. So many came up and offered their good wishes and concern for her recovery. The warmth proved a bit overwhelming. But it pleased Darcy, and that made it worthwhile.

Mr. Steadman strode up to them. "Very good to see you this morning, Mrs. Darcy."

"Good morning, sir. I know Mr. Darcy has said this already, but I must offer my thanks for your assistance. I shudder to think what might have befallen me had you not been so attentive that afternoon."

He removed his hat and held it before his chest. "Glad to be of service, madam. It is the way of Pemberley, to watch out for one another and do what we can."

"Indeed," Mrs. Steadman added. "You gave us quite a fright, finding you like that. Nothing could be a better Christmas blessing than knowing you are hale and hearty."

"I am not so sure about hearty yet," Elizabeth lifted one of her walking sticks toward them, "But I have every hope to be soon."

"We were all surprised to hear the picnic would go on as planned. Thank you for that. It means so much to the children—and their families—" she whispered behind her hand, "to know that the master and mistress are thinking of them."

"As you said," Darcy glanced at Elizabeth, "we look out for one another."

The church bell chimed again and they went into the service.

It was strange not to be heading to the baker's after Christmas service, but the ovens at Pemberley were large enough to roast the Christmas goose. So large in fact that they roasted one for the Steadmans as well.

But the goose would wait until after the picnic.

As soon as they arrived back at the manor, the party turned to Elizabeth and Aunt Gardiner for instructions. With Georgiana as her deputy, Elizabeth directed the preparations of the food tables outside. Aunt Gardiner set up the activities for the children, and Darcy and Fitzwilliam oversaw the men as they erected the canopies on the lawn.

An hour later, the children and their families arrived. The Gardiner children greeted the youngest guests as if inviting them into their own home, with all the warmth learnt from their parents. They immediately organized themselves for a game of rounders on the lawn. Uncle and Aunt joined in.

Georgiana and Mrs. Steadman brought out hoops and graces for the younger girls and cavorted around the grounds after errant hoops.

"I do not remember the last time Georgiana laughed like that." Darcy said, standing behind Elizabeth's chair.

"It is good to see her so happy."

"You wish you were playing rounders with the children, do you not?" Darcy squeezed her shoulder.

"I do."

"Then next year you shall."

"Next year?"

"Yes, I am convinced we should make this part of Pemberley's regular Christmas celebration. There is too much good cheer here not to see it repeated."

She laid her hand on her shoulder, over his. "I think your mother would approve. Her journal suggested that these were her favorite events at Pemberley"

"You would have been very fond of her and she of you."

"I have no doubt. I am very fond of her son." She smiled up at him.

Oh, how his eyes lit up when she did that. He might be a man with few words to speak, but his eyes said all that was necessary.

"And I you, Mrs. Darcy. And I you. Happy Christmas, my love." He leaned down to kiss her.

"Happy Christmas to you. Mr. Darcy."

.

⁂Regency Christmas Traditions

IF YOU WOULD LIKE to read more about Regency Era Christmas traditions, then **A Jane Austen Christmas** is just what you are looking for.. In ebook and paper-

back, you can find it at all major online book sellers.

Here's a sample to whet your appetite.

⁂

Celebrating a Jane Austen Christmas

Each year the holi-day season seems to begin earlier and earli-er. Complaints about holiday excesses and longings for 'simpler' and 'old fashioned' holiday celebrations abound. But what exactly does an 'old fashioned Christmas' really look like?

Many Christmas traditions and images of 'old fashioned' holidays are based on Victorian celebrations. Going back just a little further, to the beginning of the 19th century, the holiday Jane Austen knew would have looked distinctly odd to modern sensibilities.

How odd? Families rarely decorated Christmas trees. Festivities centered on socializing instead of gift-giving. Festivities focused on adults, with children largely consigned to the nursery. Holiday events, including balls, parties, dinners, and even weddings celebrations, started a week before Advent (the fourth Sunday before Christmas) and extended all the way through to Twelfth Night in January.

As today, not everyone celebrated the same way or observed all the same customs, but many observances were widely recognized. Some of the traditions and dates that might have been observed included:

Stir it up Sunday
On the fifth Sunday before Christmas, the family would gather to 'stir up' Christmas puddings that needed to age before serving at Christmas dinner.

December 6th: St. Nicholas Day
In a tradition from Northern Europe, the day might be celebrated with the exchange of small gifts, particularly for children. House parties and other Christmastide visiting also began on or near this day.

December 21st: St. Thomas Day

Elderly women and widows went 'thomasing' at the houses of their more fortunate neighbors, hoping for gifts of food or money. Oftentimes landowners cooked and distributed wheat, an especially expensive commodity, to the 'mumpers' who came begging.

December 24th: Christmas Eve

Holiday decorating happened on Christmas Eve when families cut or bought evergreen boughs to deck the house. The greenery remained in place until Epiphany when it was removed and burned lest it bring bad luck.

December 25th: Christmas day

Families typically began the day with a trip to church and might pick up their Christmas goose from the local baker on the way home. Though gifts were not usually exchanged on Christmas, children might receive small gifts and cottagers might give generous landowners a symbolic gift in appreciation of their kindness.

The day culminated in a much anticipated feast. Traditional foods included boar's head, brawn, roast goose, mince meat pies, and the Christmas puddings made a month earlier.

December 26th: Boxing Day

After receiving their Christmas boxes, servants usually enjoyed a rare day off. Churches distributed the money from their alms-boxes.

Families might attend the opening day of panto-mimes. The wealthy traditionally enjoyed fox hunting on this day.

THE CHRISTMAS DINNER.

~Peter Parley, *Tales about Christmas*

December 31: New Year's Eve

Families thoroughly cleaned the house before gathering in a circle before midnight to usher out the old year and in the new.

Some Scots and folks of northern England believed in 'first footing'—the first visitor to set foot across the threshold after midnight on New Year's Eve affected the family's fortunes. The 'first footer' entered through the front door and left through the back door, taking all the old year's troubles and sorrows with him.

Jan 1: New Year's Day

The events of New Year's Day predicted the fortunes for the coming year, with a variety of traditions said to discern the future like 'creaming the well', or the burning of a hawthorn bush.

Jan 6th: Twelfth Night

A feast day honoring the coming of the Magi, Epiphany or Twelfth Night, marked the traditional climax of the holiday season and the time when celebrants exchanged gifts.

Revels, masks and balls were the order of the day. With the rowdy games and large quantities of highly alcoholic punch, they became so raucous that Queen Victoria outlawed Twelfth Night parties by the 1870's.

The Joys of Plum Pudding

"Hallo! A great deal of steam! The pudding was out of the copper [boiler]. A smell like washing–day! That was the cloth [the pudding bag]. A smell like an eating house and a pastrycook's next door to each other, with a laundress's next door to that! That was the pudding!

In half a minute Mrs. Cratchit entered—flushed, but smiling proudly—with the pudding. Like a speckled cannon ball, so hard and firm, blazing in half of half-a-quartern of ignited brandy, and bedight with Christmas holly stuck into the top."

"Oh, a wonderful pudding! Bob Cratchit said, and calmly too, that he regarded it as the greatest success achieved by Mrs. Cratchit since their marriage..."

Charles Dickens~A Christmas Carol

Origins of Plum Pudding

Plum pudding stands out as one of the few foods that can trace its history back at least eight hundred years. It began in Roman times as a pottage, a meat and vegetable concoction prepared in a large cauldron, to which dried fruits, sugar and spices might be added.

Porridge or *frumenty* appeared in the 14th century. Eaten during the days preceding Christmas celebrations, the soup-like fasting dish contained meats, raisins, currants, prunes, wine and spices. By the 15th century, *plum pottage,* a soupy mix of meat, vegetables and fruit often appeared at the start of a meal.

As the 17th century opened, frumenty evolved into a plum pudding. Thickened with eggs and breadcrumbs, the addition of beer and spirits gave it more flavor and increased its shelf life. Suet gradually replaced meat in the recipe and the root vegetables disappeared.

By 1650, plum pudding had transformed from a main dish to the customary Christmas dessert. Not long afterward though, Oliver Cromwell banned plum pudding because he believed the ritual of flaming the pudding resembled pagan celebrations of the winter solstice.

George I, sometimes called the Pudding King, revived the dish in 1714 when he requested plum pudding as part of the royal feast celebrating his first Christmas in England. As a result, it regained its place in traditional holiday celebrations.

In the 1830's it took its final cannon-ball form, made with flour, fruits, suet, sugar and spices, all topped with holly and flaming brandy. Anthony Trollope's *Doctore Thorne* dubbed the dish 'Christmas Pudding' in 1858.

Preparing plum pudding

Many households had their own 'receipt' (recipe) for Christmas pudding, some handed down through families for generations. Most recipes shared a set of common ingredients: finely chopped suet, currants, raisins, and other dried fruit, eggs, flour, milk, spices and brandy. These were mixed together, wrapped in a pudding cloth and boiled four or five hours.

To enhance their flavor after cooking, Christmas puddings hung on hooks to dry out for weeks prior to serving. Once dried, wrapped in alcohol-soaked cheese cloth and placed in earthenware, cooks took the puddings somewhere cool to further age. Some added more alcohol during this period and sealed the puddings with suet or wax to aid in preservation.

Plum pudding traditions

With a food so many centuries in the making, it is not surprising that many traditions have evolved around the preparation and eating of plum pudding.

The last Sunday before Advent, falling sometime between November 20th and 26th, was considered the last day to make Christmas puddings and still give them time to age properly.

It received the moniker 'Stir-up Sunday' because the opening words of the main prayer in the Book of Common Prayer of 1549 for that day are:

"Stir-up, we beseech thee, O Lord, the wills of thy faithful people; that they, plenteously bringing forth the fruit of good works, may of thee be plenteously rewarded; through Jesus Christ our Lord. Amen."

Choir boys parodied the prayer:

"Stir up, we beseech thee, the pudding in the pot. And when we do get home tonight, we'll eat it up hot."

Tradition decrees Christmas pudding be made with thirteen ingredients to represent Christ and the twelve apostles. All family members helped in 'stirring up' the pudding with a special wooden spoon (in honor of Christ's crib.) The stirring had to be done clockwise, from east to west to honor the journey of the Magi, with eyes shut, while making a secret wish.

Some added tiny charms to the pudding. These revealed their finders' fortune. The trinkets often included a thimble for spinsterhood or thrift, a ring for marriage, a coin for wealth, a miniature horseshoe or a tiny wishbone for good luck, a shoe for travel, and an anchor for safe harbor.

At the end of the Christmas feast, the pudding made a dramatic entrance to the dining room. With a sprig of holly on top as a reminder of Jesus' Crown of Thorns and bathed in flaming brandy, representing the Passion of Christ and Jesus' love and power, the Christmas pudding leant a theatrical aspect to the celebration.

Why is it called plum pudding?

And the answer to the most burning question: Why call it 'plum pudding' when it contains no plums?

Dried plums, or prunes, were popular in pies in medieval times, but in the 16th and 17th centuries raisins replaced them. In the 17th century, plums referred to raisins or other dried fruits. The dishes made with them retain the term 'plum' to this day.

Acknowledgments

So many people have helped me along the journey taking this from an idea to a reality.

Jan, , Ruth, Anji, Julie, and Debbie thank you so much for cold reading, proof reading and being honest!

And my dear friend Cathy, my biggest cheerleader, you have kept me from chickening out more than once!

And my sweet sister Gerri who believed in even those first attempts that now live in the file drawer!

Thank you!

Other Books by

Maria Grace

Given Good Principles Series:
Darcy's Decision
The Future Mrs. Darcy
All the Appearance of Goodness
Twelfth Night at Longbourn

Remember the Past
The Darcy Brothers
A Jane Austen Christmas: Regency Christmas Traditions
Mistaking Her Character
A Spot of Sweet Tea: Hopes and Beginnings
(short story collection)
The Darcys' First Christmas

Short Stories:
Four Days in April
Sweet Ginger
Last Dance
Not Romantic
To Forget (coming late 2015)

Available in paperback, e-book, and audiobook format at all online bookstores.

MARIA GRACE

On Line Exclusives at:

www.http//RandomBitsofFascination.com

**Bonus and deleted scenes
Regency Life Series**

Free e-books:
Bits of Bobbin Lace
*The Scenes Jane Austen Never Wrote: First
Anniversaries*
*Half Agony, Half Hope: New Reflections on
Persuasion*
Four Days in April

About the Author

Though Maria Grace has been writing fiction since she was ten years old, those early efforts happily reside in a file drawer and are unlikely to see the light of day again, for which many are grateful. After penning five file-drawer novels in high school, she took a break from writing to pursue college and earn her doctorate in Educational Psychology. After 16 years of university teaching, she returned to her first love, fiction writing.

She has one husband, two graduate degrees and two black belts, three sons, four undergraduate majors, five nieces, six novels in draft form, waiting for editing, sewn seven Regency era costumes, eight published novels, , shared her life with nine cats through the years, and tries to run at least ten miles a week.

She can be contacted at:

author.MariaGrace@gmail.com

Facebook:
http://facebook.com/AuthorMariaGrace

On Amazon.com:
http://amazon.com/author/mariagrace

Random Bits of Fascination
(http://RandomBitsofFascination.com)

Austen Variations (http://AustenVariations.com)

English Historical Fiction Authors
 (http://EnglshHistoryAuthors.blogspot.com)

White Soup Press (http://whitesouppress.com/)

On Twitter @WriteMariaGrace

On Pinterest: http://pinterest.com/mariagrace423/

Made in United States
North Haven, CT
28 December 2022

30266686R00105